He had been in her mind for ten years.

Gregor's voice was deep; Elena remembered the accent so well. Too well. She could never forget it. "You are my new neighbor?" he asked.

She could speak. She *had* to speak. She had to appear normal. "Yes," she said, "my name is Elena Kingdon."

"I know," was the rather startling reply, and her heart bumped in panic. "My name is Gregor Vlados—I saw you in the hotel today. You will not have seen me, I think. I came in only briefly."

Oh, but I did, I did, she thought. You are the whole purpose of my being here, but with any luck at all you won't find that out until I'm ready to tell you....

Love's Sweet Revenge

by

MARY WIBBERLEY

Harlequin Books

TORONTO • LONDON • NEW YORK • AMSTERDAM
SYDNEY • HAMBURG • PARIS

Original hardcover edition published in 1979
by Mills & Boon Limited

ISBN 0-373-02267-0

Harlequin edition published June 1979

Printed in U.S.A.

CHAPTER ONE

ELENA was going back to the island for the first time in ten years. She had been fourteen when they left, and had thought she would never return. But time had passed, and circumstances had changed.

One thing hadn't changed. That was the hate she felt for Gregor Vlados. As she thought his name, she saw him again in her mind's eye, tall, dark, and powerful. He would be ten years older now, thirty-five or near, and he too might be different. He certainly wouldn't recognise her. She had been a skinny fourteen-year-old with glasses, pigtails, and a brace on her teeth, and she had stood at the window and watched him pass with tears in her eyes and hatred in her heart, because he had nearly killed her mother and ruined her father. They had gone back to England then, and she had never seen him again. But soon she would. She hadn't planned her revenge yet, but she would know, when she met him —and then, then—she would decide.

The plane dipped and banked in a wide circle as it approached the island, and Elena checked her seat belt as the notice came on. She wondered if there would be anyone to meet her at the airstrip. There had been enough advance publicity, her publisher had seen to that. He had sent her the cut-

tings from the local newspapers, and she had read
them, seen photographs of herself, and smiled. The
smile was one of satisfaction mingled with pain.
Satisfaction because she was so vastly different from
the unhappy teenager who had left Cristobál Island;
pain because she had never intended to come back.

They were about to land. She looked in her handbag mirror, saw the face that looked back at her,
smooth-skinned, gently oval, with dark-lashed blue
eyes and a smooth cap of shining dark brown hair
and a softly curved, deceptively gentle mouth, and
she was pleased. No, he definitely wouldn't recognise her. She was beautiful now. She knew it, accepted it as a fact of her successful life, just as she
accepted the fact that men flocked round her like
the bees round a honey-pot and had done since the
age of sixteen when she had taken the teeth-brace
off for the last time, exchanged the spectacles for
contact lenses, and discovered she had a figure. She
had also, two years previously, discovered that she
could write books that sold. She had written stories
ever since childhood, she had even, at the age of
fifteen, attempted a book. The stories had sold,
the book hadn't. And then, three years ago, she had
read a top-selling historical romance, decided she
could do better—and proved it. That first book had
now been turned into a film, she had written two
more that were selling all over the world, and she
was researching her fourth.

The saddest thing of all was that her success had
come too late for her father to see. He would have

loved it, but he had died before she had had her first book accepted. She braced herself as the plane touched down, and watched from the porthole with eyes that were suddenly blurred as the runway sped past. 'Damn!' she breathed. She didn't want to get out of the plane sniffling like a child. She was cool, assured, self-possessed, a successful writer. She took a deep breath and willed the tears to disappear.

The next minute the doors were opened and the stewardess was ushering the passengers off the plane. Elena waited quietly until the shuffling people had passed, then she gathered her hand luggage and walked down the aisle. The stewardess smiled warmly at her. 'It looks as if you have a welcoming committee waiting, Miss Kingdon,' she said.

Elena gave her what she hoped was a modest, rueful smile. 'Oh dear,' she said. 'I wondered——' she took a peep outside to where a group of people clustered at the foot of the steps, several men, a couple of women, and a girl with a bouquet of flowers. She recognised one of the men as Jerry Arnold, her American publisher. Good old Jerry! He'd brought a couple of photographers too. They stood a few feet away, cameras at the ready, slightly bored.

'Here I go,' she winked at the friendly stewardess. 'Want to get your photo in the papers?'

'Why not? Shall I lead the way?'

They went down smiling, and bulbs flashed, and Jerry came forward to take her hand and kiss her on the cheek, and murmur: 'Hello, honey.'

He had fallen in love with her the minute he'd

met her two years previously. She was fond of him, no more, and he knew it, and was resigned to the fact. It didn't stop him pursuing her wherever, whenever he was able. She was introduced to one or two local notables, the little girl curtsied and presented the bouquet, Elena said her goodbyes to the stewardess, was whisked through Customs at V.I.P. speed, and a few minutes later was sitting in the back of an air-conditioned Rolls with Jerry.

'You certainly do things in style,' she told him, smiling gently at him. 'Thanks.'

'I'm still not sure why you wanted a fuss,' he grumbled. 'You've never wanted one before——'

'I've not been to Cristobál before,' she answered, hating the necessary lie, but it had to be so. 'And I thought—why not? It's time I got some publicity.'

'You've got another reason,' he remarked.

'Have I?' she raised her eyebrows. Jerry was shrewd, far shrewder than his casual, unkempt appearance admitted.

'Mmm, yes. But I can't decide what it is.'

'You just concentrate on promoting my books,' she patted his hand, 'and we'll all be happy.'

'You'd be happier still if you married me,' he said, looking at her fondly.

'Ah, but you might not. We writers are temperamental—or hadn't you heard?'

'I deal with enough, I should know—but you're not, my sweet. You are the most delicious person I've ever met.'

'Am I?' her eyes were laughing. 'But I'm too

young. I've decided not to get married until I'm at least thirty—and until I've written another five books.'

'And made me a millionaire in the process? You're so kind, Elena,' but he was laughing now. They both knew his proposals were a regular thing, and perhaps not to be taken too seriously.

'Where are we going?' she asked.

'A small lunch at one of Cristobál's larger hotels with our friends in the following car, then I'll take you to your house and let you settle in. I have to fly back to the States tomorrow, but I'll be back at the weekend.'

She sat back. She had checked up on Gregor Vlados and knew he still lived on the island, in the house that had belonged to her parents, but more than that she had not been able to discover. She might, if she was careful, find out something about him over the lunch.

She could wait. She had waited for ten years, another day was not too much to ask. They were entering the town now, and it was all so familiar, all so much the same as it had always been that she felt a stab of apprehension. Would the pain and anguish flood back too? She didn't know. She was no longer the gauche child who had left here with a broken heart, she was a woman, confident, beautiful, but memories were nearly overwhelming.

'——and this is San Cristobál, the capital population—er—um—oh, around twenty thousand, I guess, and the main industry is sugar, bananas, coffee, copra——' Jerry's voice, delivering his tourist guide commentary, washed around her. She already knew it all. She had lived here. But he didn't know that, so she nodded, and pretended to listen, and saw the tall, beautiful white buildings of the town centre, the wide streets thronged with natives and tourists from cruise liners, the market place—the biggest tourist attraction of all—jammed with people, and she suddenly knew to which hotel they were going. They were near it now, and the name could be seen, neon emblazoned on the front, so it was safe enough to ask: 'Are we lunching at the Plaza?'

'Yep.' He looked behind them. They appeared to have lost the following car in the heavy lunchtime traffic. 'Damn, they've vanished.'

'Never mind. It will give me time to put some make-up on.'

'You don't need it,' he assured her. 'You're gorgeous as you are.'

'Please!' She lowered her eyes in mock modesty. 'You'll make me blush, sir.'

'How you can be so lovely *and* brainy I'll never know.'

Elena looked surprised. 'Oh, didn't you know? The books write themselves. I just sit down, put pen to paper, and it all happens—at least that's what one journalist who interviewed me last week seemed to think. So I told her, very sweetly I thought, to go and try one and let me see the first chapter when she'd done it. I bet I never hear from her again.'

Jerry laughed. 'I'll bet you don't!' He caught her hand in his. 'I'm going to spend as much time with you as I can, while you're here.'

'I'm *writing*, love—working. I won't have a lot of time. Anyway, how will they manage in New York without you? You do have other authors, you know —or have you been conning me all this time? Am I your only writer?'

He laughed, amused at that. 'You know darn well you're not. You're certainly the best looking, though.' The car drew up outside the ornate front of the hotel, and Jerry helped her out, and into the cool, air-conditioned lobby, where a bowing manager welcomed them in fractured English.

Half an hour later, Elena was sitting eating at a large round table with Jerry and the others. She was used to this type of lunch, where all she had to do was listen, look pleasant and charming, ask a few odd questions about the beautiful island she was on so that they would go away and tell everyone else that Elena Kingdon was really a delightful woman. She was sitting next to the mayor's wife, because she spoke the best English. She was a large fussy woman with flashing eyes and jet black hair and too much jewellery—but she also possessed a shrewd wit, and had managed, in between the general chit-chat all round, to give Elena potted biographies of several other lunchers in the dining room—biographies that, if their owners could have heard, might have caused them to leave hastily in some confusion.

Elena repressed a laugh at one outrageous account about the life and manners of an elderly bald-headed man who was sitting at a discreet corner table with a young woman. She looked across at him and shook her head. 'Amazing,' she murmured. 'He looks so—respectable, somehow.'

'My dear,' Madame Rossi whispered, 'it is all true, every word.' She looked at Elena. 'If he asks you to one of his parties, make some excuse.'

'Oh, I will,' Elena reassured her, 'and thanks for warning me. Life is never dull here, is it?' They were interrupted by a comment of Jerry's, then the waiters came to clear the plates, and they settled down to order their dessert.

And then it happened. Elena looked up from the menu, because there seemed to be a slight disturbance at the entrance to the dining room—and she saw a man standing there, and he was looking across at her and the years rolled back and she thought she would die. The man was Gregor Vlados. He had changed, but not all that much. He had filled out. The youth was now the man, a tall man, over six feet tall, broad-shouldered, dressed in tight cream trousers and dark blue open-necked shirt showing the black hair on his chest. But it was his face that riveted Elena. She literally could not look away for a few explosive seconds. She had not expected to see him so soon—and the shock was all the greater for that. The tanned Slavic face with high cheekbones and square chin had not altered, nor had his raven black hair, shaggy, over-long. But his eyes held the knowledge of years, and it was from them she could not look away. Deep, dark grey eyes, narrowed now as if he waited for something—she knew not what. Broad straight nose, wide cynical mouth, faintly curved as if he were about to smile. But he didn't. He turned and spoke to the waiter by his side, and the spell was broken. Elena felt the perspiration break out on her brow. Gregor Vlados, the man who had ruined her father, and in so doing caused her mother's death, was the most stunningly attractive man she had ever seen in her life.

'And *that*,' said Madame Rossi in a strange voice, 'is Gregor Vlados, one of the most powerful men on the island.' Her voice seemed to come from far away. Elena took a deep breath, fighting for calm after the shock.

'Oh? He's very good-looking.' The words were banal, but at least they came out almost normally. Gregor had turned, was going out. Elena said the next, absurd thing that entered her head. 'Don't tell me they've turned him away because he's not wearing a tie?' It was a ridiculous thing to say. Half the men in the room—including Jerry—wore open-necked shirts, but her wits were blunted by the strange encounter.

Madame Rossi chuckled, highly amused. 'He *owns* the hotel, my dear. I would imagine he came only to look at you—the famous author.'

That had been the first shock. But there were more to come, and the second came as the evening drew in, and the air became cooler, and Elena sat by a window in her new house and looked over the magnificently colourful garden, filled with a rich profusion of flowers in so many colours and hues that the eye was dazzled.

Jerry had left her alone to settle in while he made some telephone calls to the States from his hotel. He would be back to take her out to wine and dine, he had said. She had let him go gladly. She needed to be alone to think, and until then had had no opportunity. She had looked all round the house —her house—which was small and beautiful, with a housekeeper hired by Jerry, and her husband, the gardener living out, and a fridge packed full of food. From her bedroom she could see the sea, and over the horizon to the west was Mexico. The island itself was situated in the Gulf of Mexico, within easy plane distance of the United States and the Bahamas. An ideal climate, a beautiful place to live, and her parents had brought her and her brother here as small children when they had left the South of France so suddenly, because Elena's father's brother —Elena's godfather—lived here. It was he who had left her this house when he had died six months ago. And it was that fact which had decided her to come stay while she wrote a book—and get her revenge on Gregor Vlados. Jerry only knew that the house had been left her by a distant relative. She had not told him it was her uncle, she had implied some very remote, elderly cousin. In a way it was not a lie, for they had never been close. Something else must have happened at that dreadful time ten years ago, for all connections with Uncle Jim had been severed when they left, and the bequest of the house had been, for Elena, one of the biggest surprises of her life.

She sat now, gazing over the rapidly darkening gardens, and she was back in the past, in that other house where they had lived, which now belonged to Gregor Vlados, recalling the brief snatch of conversation she had overheard which had in a way started the nightmare. Elena had been passing the lounge on her way to the kitchen for a cool drink, padding silently, barefoot because it was so hot, when her father's voice from the lounge had made her pause, fearful, apprehensive, because there had been something dreadful in it.

'Gregor Vlados—is here.'

Her mother had answered: 'How do you know it's him? It could be——'

'It's him all right. I wonder how——'

'You don't think——' her mother's voice sounded faint, as if she was clutching her throat, as she did when she was nervous.

'*No!*' And then he had seen Elena through the open doorway.

'What is it?' she had asked.

'Nothing, love. Nothing.' He had come to the door, and his face was white and strained.

'B-but you said——'

'It's nothing to concern yourself with,' he had answered.

But it had been, because, six months later, when

they had left the island for good, her mother was dying, and her father was a shadow of the man he had been. And they had no money. Elena knew that the man responsible was the man she had seen today, because her father had told her so. She had never forgotten or forgiven.

She didn't want to sit there any longer. The housekeeper, Señora Bonita, a small plump Mexican woman, had left after telling Elena she would be back in the morning, and had gone to the cottage nearby that Uncle Jim had had built for his staff. Jerry might be another hour, she knew his phone calls, having been on the receiving end of several. Time meant nothing to him. Picking up her stole from the chair, for the air had grown noticeably cooler, Elena opened the french windows and stepped outside on to the stone patio. In the distance a sprinkler whirled. Señor Bonita had assured her he would switch it off later.

She stepped on to the faintly damp grass and began to walk towards the trees that bordered the garden. Her eyes grew accustomed to the dark as she walked along, and the shadows held no fears for her. She enjoyed the dusk, and at home in England often used to take her neighbour's dog for walks in the park, or on the common during late evening. It was a time when ideas flowed more freely, and she had quite often come home, handed the dog back to her neighbour and dashed up to her flat to write down everything that had come to her before it vanished.

But there was a difference, here. She paused by a

stone sundial set squarely in the middle of the slop-
ing lawn. In England she had been able to put all
thoughts of Gregor Vlados out of her mind for
weeks, even months at a time. Her life was crammed to capacity with writing, researching in libra-
ries and bookshops, and meeting her friends—
mainly writers, some successful, some not, but all
living in the same little world of books, publishers,
manuscripts—and mutual encouragement.

And now, at last, she was away from it all. She was
here to write her best book yet—and suddenly she
wasn't sure if she would be able to. Might thoughts
of him not intrude? She was able to shut her mind
off completely from the outside world when she
wrote, to the extent of literally not hearing the telephone if it rang—but she had lived with him in her
mind, at the back of it, for ten years. And today,
only hours ago, she had seen him again. The reality
had been different from the image she had carried.
The picture engraved in her mind had been of a
young man in his twenties, hard-faced, hard-eyed,
ruthless. Today she seen the man he had become—
and even now could recall the shock and sudden
awareness, and relive it. And the difference was in
the maturity, and the aura of sheer strength around
him. What was it Madame Rossi had said? 'Gregor
Vlados, one of the most powerful men on the island.'
Elena didn't doubt it.

She reached the trees. It was a mere line of them,
screening a garden from hers, and then she saw the
house, lit up, at the other side, and she went dizzy

for a moment. She had not known, she had not re-membered. The house she saw now was the one she had lived in. She closed her eyes, suddenly icily cold, and unable to move.

Then a dark shape bounded out of the trees, and a man's voice shouted: 'Negra!' and she screamed, because for one moment she seemed to see a black panther leaping at her. She stumbled and nearly fell, and a man's deep voice said: 'I am sorry,' and she saw the dark silhouette of him as he came quickly forward to catch her arm, as the dog—it was a dog, not a panther—whined softly and lay down a few feet away. And she saw that the man was Gregor Vlados.

CHAPTER TWO

GREGOR'S voice was deep, Elena remembered the accent so well. Too well. She could never forget it. It was the same. She jerked her arm free, because his touch was fire, and he said:

'He would not hurt you.' Then a pause, and she saw something alter in his face, shadowy though it was. 'You are my new neighbour?'

She could speak. She *had* to speak. She had to appear normal.

'Yes. My name is Elena Kingdon.' She had taken her mother's maiden name when she began writing, and altered the spelling of her christian name. Elena Kingdon looked better on a book cover than Eleanor Shaw.

'I know,' was the rather startling reply, and her heart bumped in panic. 'My name is Gregor Vlados —I saw you at the hotel today when you were having lunch. You will not have seen me, I think, I came in only briefly.'

Oh, but I did, I did, she thought. You are the whole purpose of my being here, but with any luck you won't find that out until I'm ready to tell you. She managed to smile. It was quite an effort, but she hadn't schooled herself and learnt self-control for nothing. 'I'm sorry I panicked just then,' she said, 'but he is rather large—I thought I was being attacked by a wild animal.'

'Negra, here!' The man spoke, and the dog rose obediently and walked to stand between them, looking up at his master as if waiting further instructions. 'This lady is a friend. And this is her garden.' The dog wagged his tail and looked up at Elena as if he understood. She bent down to pat his head.

'Please, come and have a drink at my house. It is the only way I can apologise for your fright.'

Her decision took only a split second. 'Thank you.' Gregor pushed back a branch that might have caught her hair, and she went through the narrow gap to emerge into his garden. It was all happening too quickly, much too quickly.

'This way, there are some steps here.' He touched her arm briefly, to guide her, and she had to make a strong effort not to flinch, but she succeeded. I know these steps, she thought, I've walked up them so many times, and I know your house too, and if I can walk in without crying I know I'll have won the first round. The dog padded silently in after them and Elena walked through open french windows into the lounge where she had heard that fateful, life-changing conversation. Her face was calm. She showed nothing of the turmoil inside her. The room was completely different now, of course—light modern furniture, beautiful rugs on the black-tiled floor, and a picture on the wall that she recognised as a Gauguin original. It oozed wealth, but not ostentatiously. The chairs were of cane, high round

backed, peacock style, and there was a long low
settee covered in pale green silk. A large round onyx
table matched the cover of the settee, and on it stood
a crystal vase full of flowers. It was a man's room, yet
it had a woman's touch in the flowers, and in the
small flower-embroidered cushions on the settee.

'Please, sit down,' Gregor said. 'What would you
like to drink?'

'Anything cool.' Elena sat on the settee and looked
around her. She would not look at him, not yet.
There was plenty of time for that, all the time in
the world.

'A long dry Martini with ice and lemon?' he suggested.

She looked at him then. 'That would be perfect.'
She had seen enough in the hotel, but she hadn't
seen him close to. My God, she thought unwillingly,
he is devastating. His eyes were the most fascinating
part of him, as grey and bleak as a Siberian sky before snowfall—appropriate considering his Russian
ancestry. It was at that moment that the idea came
to her, and it was so startling and shattering that she
jerked her head back, stunned, and he frowned,
paused in the act of opening a drink cabinet, and
said:

'Is something the matter?'

'No,' she lied. 'Something flew in my eye.' She put
her hand to it to add credence to the lie, and he put
the glass down, came to her, and bent down over
her.

'Please—let me see.'

She hadn't expected that, and the idea was still so vivid that she meekly took her hand away and blinked up at him. 'I think—it's gone,' she said. He put his left hand under her chin and tilted her face up. She wanted to scream. Then he crouched in front of her, his knees touching hers, a mere brushing of them, and she felt stifled and panicky.

'It's all——' she began.

'Stay still.' The hand under her chin was a gentle one, but she felt its muscular strength. Then with his right hand Gregor lifted her left eyelid and stared hard. His face was a blur because her eyes had filled with tears——

'Oh, my God!' she gasped.

'Have I hurt you?'

'No. Oh——' she pushed him away, then said, illogically: 'Don't move.' He straightened slowly, clearly a puzzled man. 'My lens,' she said. 'I've lost it.'

'I'm sorry, I don't understand.' But he stood very still.

'My contact lens.' He was well and truly blurred now; Elena was shortsighted. She closed her left eye and began to search the front of her dress.

'Wait,' he said. 'I think I see it.' He bent down again and lifted something very carefully from the long skirt of her dress. 'Is this it?'

She took it from him. 'Thank you. Can I go to the bathroom? I want to rinse it.'

'Please—this way.' He led her out and pointed to the cloakroom by the front door. Elena fled. She locked the door, rinsed the lens and put it back in place. Then she stood by the bowl and looked at herself in the mirror above it. 'You idiot,' she told herself. But it wasn't the most important thing. The idea had taken hold and she could scarcely wait to get back to her own house and make notes. It was so simple. All the best ideas were.

In a few days she would be starting her fourth book. It was set in Russia before the time of the Revolution. She had brought several books with her, and Jerry was bringing more for her this evening. She had studied the background extensively so that she was already steeped in the atmosphere of the Russian Court in 1900 with its intrigues and plots—but until now, just a few minutes ago, there was one character who had refused to emerge clearly: Count Igor Vassily, man of intrigue, spy, seducer—the villain of the piece. But now, now she had him. She would use Gregor Vlados as a ready-made character. She would describe him, his mannerisms, she would watch and note, and the personality would grow from that, and it might help exorcise some of the bitterness she had carried in her heart to get him down on paper. And she would make his end even more gory than she had planned, and that might do some good too.

She opened the door and went back to where he waited, seated on the settee. He stood up as she went in, and handed her a long glass in which dry Martini clinked with ice. 'Is all well now?' he asked.

'Yes, thanks.' She smiled at him as she sat down. 'Cheers.'

'Cheers.' He raised his own glass. She looked at him, visualising him in the clothes of 1900. It wasn't difficult. He wore a white long-sleeved shirt unbuttoned half way revealing the mat of dark hair covering his chest, and fawn pants, exquisitely cut, showing his hard muscular thighs to perfection. He needed only high boots and a gunbelt to complete the alteration. There was a gleam of gold at his chest, and to cover the confusion of being caught looking, for he was smiling slightly, Elena said:

'Is that a medallion you wear?'

'This?' he lifted it carelessly, a heavy gold chain at the bottom of which was a small gold crucifix, exquisitely marked. She stood up.

'May I see?' She took it in her hand. It was clearly very old, and the gold had a faintly rose colour, and the design of intertwined leaves and flowers was delicately wrought in the metal. For some reason she was very moved.

'It's beautiful.'

'My grandmother gave it to me when I was a boy,' he said. 'I have always worn it, ever since.' He smiled faintly. 'Perhaps it is not, strictly speaking, a man's, but no one has ever remarked on that.'

She thought—would they dare? She wanted to move away from him, from the sheer masculinity of him. It almost made her tingle, the nearness, the sheer animal virility that he exuded. She turned, picked up her glass from the table, and sipped the icy drink.

'Tell me,' he said, 'for how long do you plan to stay here on the island?'

'I'm writing a book,' she answered. 'For as long as it takes me. Perhaps six months or so. I bought the house——' that was part of her story, only Jerry knew—— 'so that I could have the peace and quiet to write in.'

'I see. And is the book set here?'

'No. It's set in Russia, about 1900.'

'Really? My parents came from Russia before the war. I was born in France.' I know you were, she thought, silently. I know everything about you, I've made it my business to.

'How interesting! I knew by your name that you weren't English—or Mexican,' she smiled gently, 'but I didn't realise you were Russian. I don't suppose you have any books?'

'Several, but not perhaps of the time you want.' He shrugged. 'However, I do have a library. Please use it when you wish.'

'You're very kind.' It really was getting easier as she went along, to talk to him, not to feel physically repelled—or disturbed—by him. And she had forgotten all about Jerry. Her mind was racing ahead, planning, seeking ways—it was Jerry's voice which brought her back. Jerry calling her name loudly.

'Oh!' she looked at Gregor. 'That's my publisher.' She swallowed her drink as he went over to the window and shouted:

'She is here!'

A few moments later Jerry emerged from the trees and Elena watched him cross the lawn. 'Mind the steps,' called Gregor, and Jerry, swearing faintly in the darkness, found them.

'I've been looking everywhere——' he began accusingly, then to Gregor: 'Hi!'

'Hello. I am sorry, it is my fault Miss Kingdon is here——'

'Jerry, meet Gregor Vlados. Mr Vlados, my publisher Jerry Arnold.'

The two men shook hands, Gregor said: 'May I offer you a drink?'

'Well——' Jerry looked doubtfully at Elena, who nodded faintly.

'Okay, thanks, I will. Same as you, please.' He looked round him in approval. 'It's a nice house you have here, Mr Vlados.'

'Thank you.' Gregor handed him a drink.

'Thanks. Is—er—Mrs Vlados about?'

'I am not married.'

The expression on Jerry's face was almost comical—dismay, quickly covered by embarrassment, followed by a look Elena knew only too well. Hastily she said: 'Mr Vlados has just been offering me the use of his library if I need any books about Russia.'

'But you won't, honey. Wait till you see the pile

I brought over. I've left them in the lounge.'

'That's very kind of you, Jerry.'

'Tell me,' asked Gregor, 'do you look after all Miss Kingdon's business interests for her?'

'I sure do.' Jerry looked at Elena and grinned. 'She needs me, don't you, honey?'

'I don't know how I'd manage without you.'

'That is most interesting. Yet you are American, and Miss Kingdon is English.'

'That's it. But her books sell like hot cakes all over the U.S. first, then we sell to England.'

'Fascinating.' He looked interested too. Either it was genuine, or he was a good actor, Elena couldn't be sure which. But she found herself watching him as he produced cigars and offered Jerry one. 'Tell me, if I wrote a book would you be able to sell it for me?'

'You're a writer? No kidding!' Jerry's face broadened into a smile. He had met too many people, at too many parties, who were going to write a book, one day, 'when they had time,' to fall over himself with enthusiasm. He leant forward to allow Gregor to light his cigar, and Elena, now vaguely confused, watched. There was something here she didn't quite understand.

'Not a writer—no. But I have written several chapters of something already.' Gregor smiled gently, and his hard face softened, and Elena thought: I don't believe it.

'Then would you like to get them? I'd certainly

be delighted to look—but I must warn you first. You'll get an honest comment from me—and you might throw us out.'

Gregor laughed. Elena had never heard him laugh before. It was deep, attractive—genuinely amused. 'I promise, whatever you say, I will not do that,' he said. 'Excuse me.'

They were alone. Jerry looked at Elena. 'Jeez,' he groaned, 'what have I done? I'm smoking his cigar and drinking his drink, so I'll have to be tactful. But get ready to scram!' Then he frowned. 'And I'm not sure I like *him* being your neighbour.'

That was almost funny. But then Jerry didn't know. Gregor returned with a pile of paper and handed it to Jerry. 'I shall show Miss Kingdon the library,' he said, 'while you read.'

He ushered Elena out, across the hall to the room that had once been her playroom, together with her brother. Now it was lined with filled bookshelves, and had a large desk by the window. 'Please browse for as long as you wish, any time,' he said. 'I hope I can be of help.'

No doubt about it, he had a certain charm. If she hadn't hated him she could have found herself attracted to the dark good looks of him. She turned away, lest her thoughts show.

'Thank you,' she said. It was easier to stand with her back to him, running her fingers along the profusion of books, than make conversation. He had a fantastic collection, no doubt about it. The classics were there, and modern authors, and history and archaeology rubbed shoulders with books on hotel management, books in Russian, in French, in Spanish——

'Do you speak many languages?' she asked.

'Only four, as you see. But I prefer to read in English.'

'I see.' She stood back. 'There's really too much for me to take in at once.'

'Then you shall come back, of course. Come,' he opened the door, 'we will see what your friend makes of my efforts.'

Elena hoped Jerry hated it, and would tell him so, but Jerry possessed too much tact. Then she saw his face when she walked in the other room, and something struck her, almost like a physical blow. He was holding the papers. He was engrossed. And he looked up, not at Elena, at Gregor.

'My God, Mr Vlados,' he said. 'I was going to be polite, because I'm a guest in your house. But I can tell you now, I don't need to be.' He stood up slowly, and faced them. 'I've only had time to skim through, but I've read enough to know you've got an absolute stunner there. This is all true, isn't it?'

'Yes,' Gregor answered very quietly. 'It is my life story.'

'And you've never written before?'

'No. I began a couple of months ago when— something decided me to.'

Jerry shook his head. He looked stunned. 'All I can say is—please, finish it as soon as you can, get it typed—and send it to me. Better still, I'll come here for it.' He smiled at Elena. 'Honey, would you mind if I talked a while longer with Mr Vlados?'

It was all going wrong. Something strange and awful was happening, and Elena, for once, didn't know what to do about it. But she did know that she felt, suddenly, very frightened.

'I'll go and finish unpacking,' she said, 'and have a shower.'

'I will see you across the garden,' said Gregor, and before she could refuse, he called the sleeping dog and went over to the french windows. Jerry had forgotten her already. He had sat down again and was buried in the closely handwritten sheets on his knee. Outside, Elena said:

'I can manage——'

'Perhaps, but it is night. When you have finished your jobs, phone me and I will come over for you.'

'I don't need——'

'The number is 782. Just pick up and dial, and I will come.'

He held back the branches for her, and she followed, and into her own garden. Negra ran ahead, barking, and Gregor touched her arm lightly.

'Did you leave a door open?'

'Yes—I only intended being out a few minutes——'

'That was foolish. I will come in with you and look around. We have little crime here, but it is wise to close doors and downstairs windows at night.'

Elena was getting fed up with him, and obscurely

angry with herself—and Jerry. Jerry, who professed to love her yet had been so engrossed in reading something this man had written that she might as well not have been there. 'I'll check when I get in,' she replied coldly. 'I don't scare easily——'

'Except when you see a dog, perhaps?'

She stopped and turned on him. Negra had run ahead into the house, and had stopped barking. 'Are you trying to be funny? I don't find that remark amusing at all. I could hardly know——'

'That he wasn't dangerous? No.' Was he laughing at her? She felt her temper rising and clenched her fists to stop herself from striking him. She didn't want to touch him.

'You can leave me here,' she managed to say. 'And *thank* you for seeing me this far.'

'I insist on coming in.' He walked ahead and left her. The house was in darkness. Elena saw light flood out, and walked slowly on.

She could hear the dog running round upstairs, and Gregor had gone too. She looked round the room. Nothing had been touched, even her handbag was still on the chair. It had been rather silly to leave everything, but she had only intended walking in her own garden. She heard footsteps, and Gregor came in, filling the room with power. 'It is safe,' he said. 'All is well. Negra, sit.' The dog sat down obediently by his feet.

'If you prefer I will leave Negra here, and he can accompany you back,' he said, and said something quietly to the animal.

'Very well.' She didn't want to return to his house, but she didn't appear to have much choice. Her first evening on the island, she was supposed to be going out with Jerry, and he had been taken over by this man, her evening. She didn't want them to be alone together for too long. Gregor was clever. He might find out things she would prefer him not to know—not yet anyway. 'I shan't be long. Jerry and I intend to go out.'

'And I do not wish to detain you. As soon as you are ready, of course, I will let him go.' He nodded and walked out. But it's not a question of you letting him go, she thought, it's Jerry who wants to talk.

The dog made as if to move, and she said softly: 'Stay,' and he subsided, looked up at her, and wagged his tail. He really was a beautiful animal, large and sleek-furred, a mixture of labrador and heaven knew what else. She stooped to stroke him, and he rolled over on his back, paws in the air. She knew what that meant, and tickled his chest and stomach. 'You're just a big softie,' she said, and he closed his eyes as if in agreement. But he wasn't. He looked as tough as his master, and she didn't doubt he could be when necessary. She stood up. 'You stay here,' she told him. 'I won't be long.'

She decided to finish her unpacking the following morning; she would have a shower, change, and go back. She felt vaguely uneasy about Jerry being there with the big Russian. Shrewd he might be, but he could well say something innocently that could cause Gregor to think—perhaps to wonder who she really was.

She selected a cool white long dress in swirly silk that clung to her figure in a flattering way. It was one of her favourites, low-necked, sleeveless, and she wore only a jade pendant on a chain with it. She showered, dressed, slipped on her gold sandals, transferred keys and hanky to a gold evening purse, smoothed on a little lipstick, and went down to find Negra waiting.

She checked all doors and windows, left on the lounge light, and went out of the front door, round to the back, and across the garden, the dog padding silently ahead of her. Quietly she crossed into Gregor's garden, up the stone steps, and paused. She could hear men's laughter from the open windows of Gregor's lounge, then a low murmur of voices, and more sudden laughter. Puzzled, she moved nearer, very quietly, and realised they were telling jokes. Her mouth tightened. Jerry had stayed behind to talk about writing—and now they were like a couple of schoolboys telling jokes—probably smutty ones, judging by the roars of laughter that followed a whispered pause. She went towards the window, tapped lightly on it, and walked in. The two men looked round, Jerry with a slightly guilty expression, then both stood up. They both had a glass and a cigar in their hands.

'You look beautiful,' said Jerry. 'Honey, you are gorgeous.'

Gregor looked at her, and a smile touched his

mouth. 'Have you planned where you are going this evening?' he asked. Perversely, Elena was piqued. She had expected him to agree with Jerry. Not that she cared, of course——

'No. Can you recommend anywhere? The Plaza was fine for lunch, but I thought somewhere different——' Jerry paused. He didn't know Gregor owned it, and she waited for Gregor to tell him, but he didn't.

'Then I can recommend a night club that's good. It may have a lot of tourists there, at the casino, but,' he shrugged gracefully, 'you can have a drink in peace at one of the smaller bars.'

'Sounds fine. We can have a flutter, hey, Elena? Say——' he looked apologetically at Gregor, 'would you like to come? That's if you're not doing anything.' Elena looked stonily at him. Enough was enough.

Then she saw that Gregor was watching her. He smiled as if he knew. 'Perhaps not. What is the saying? Two's company——'

'Aw, come on, Elena would love you to, wouldn't you, Elena?' And she sensed what was in Gregor's mind. She knew it as though it was her own mind. It was frightening.

'Yes, of course,' she said, and smiled at Gregor as if she would have suggested it, if Jerry hadn't. 'Please come—anyway, you can guide us there, can't you?'

'Very well. Please give me a moment to change my shirt. Help yourself to drinks.' Gregor went out and Jerry looked at her, puzzled.

'What gives?' he whispered.

'Nothing. I'm tired. I don't want to be out too late, that's all.'

'Sorry, honey. I'll see to it. But I want that book of his. I *want* it badly.' He smiled at her. 'It's the businessman in me, I guess, but what a fantastic coincidence, him being your neighbour, *and* writing a book. Unbelievable!'

Unbelievable. Elena went and poured herself a stiff vodka and tonic; she needed it. It was a fantastic coincidence. She remembered something she had glimpsed briefly on Gregor's face when he and Jerry had started speaking. Something so fleeting that it might have been her imagination. But ultimately disturbing. Of course it was coincidence. She drank deeply, and felt immediately better. She could watch him while they were at this night club, and tonight, when she was home again, she would make her notes.

Gregor steered the grey Silver Shadow into a parking spot and switched off the engine. They were outside a long low building bursting with light and noise. It had not been on the island ten years ago. The neon sign flashed on and off. 'The Brown Derby', it said. 'Someone has a sense of humour,' murmured Jerry as they followed Gregor into the brightly lit entrance hall, 'did you see that brown derby perched on the roof?'

The place was crowded, and to their left they

could see the green tables of a gaming room. Ahead a subtly lit bar, to the right a restaurant. Gregor nodded, and a man rushed over to him. 'Mr Vlados, sir!' he exclaimed. 'You didn't ring——'

'I've brought two guests, Sandro,' said Gregor. 'We'll have a drink first, I think, then perhaps a game.'

'In your room?'

'No, the bar.' He turned to Elena and Jerry. 'Would you like a drink now?'

'Sure.' As they walked into the bar with low comfortable seats and tables dotted around, a white-coated waiter appeared from nowhere and bowed. 'First round's on me,' said Jerry. 'What'll it be, Elena—Gregor?'

Gregor smiled. 'All the drinks are on the house tonight.'

Elena looked at him, and she knew then. It took Jerry a moment longer.

'Gregor?' he asked. 'Is—is this——'

'Yes, I own it. Forgive me my little joke. It seemed appropriate to celebrate your enthusiasm about my writing efforts, so—as I say, the drinks are on the house. Please, what would you like?'

'It's the kind of joke I appreciate,' murmured Jerry, looking round him in a dazed kind of way. 'I'll have a vodka. I need it.'

'Elena?'

'Vodka and tonic, please.' He ushered her to a seat, the waiter bowed and vanished, and she glanced at Gregor, who sat beside her. He had ruined her father. Had he perhaps bought this place as a result of his dishonesty? She felt almost ill.

And he had called her Elena. Somehow she found that nearly as disturbing.

CHAPTER THREE

JERRY had been completely won over. The process had begun at Gregor's house, and it was now complete. Elena sat very calm and still, and sipped her drink and picked an olive out of the dish on the table, and she listened to the men talking. And all the time she was watching Gregor's every move, mentally noting down his mannerisms, observing the way he spoke to others—and seeing the way they responded to him. Some vague part of her plan faded, and was gone. She had come to the island as a celebrity, a well-known writer, prepared to find out all she could about him, prepared to use her success if she could as a weapon against him—but she had not been prepared for the undoubted fact that he was not only one of the most powerful men on the island, he must also be one of the most popular. He knew everyone there, and they knew him. And she saw the looks on their faces when he spoke to them. The men clearly warmed to him—with the women it was different, oh, so very different. She had seen something similar on Madame Rossi's face, heard it in her voice at lunch. He affected the women in a certain way. They responded, they looked at him, and it was in their eyes. How could they be so stupid? she thought, as she saw him go over to speak to a couple who had just come in.

He shook hands with the man, and kissed the woman's hand and she fluttered girlishly, like a lovesick teenager, and Elena herself felt sick. 'Boy, he's got something,' said Jerry, watching him.

'Don't tell me *you* fancy him!' snapped Elena, and he gaped at her.

'Sorry, did I say the wrong thing? He's a fantastic personality.'

'So it seems,' she said shortly.

Jerry frowned. 'Do you want to leave, honey?' he said quietly.

'Yes.' She knew she was being childish and bad-tempered, but she couldn't help it. Her crack at Jerry was inexcusable, but she didn't feel like apologising. And she was tired.

'Okay, I'll tell him.'

Contrite, Elena put her hand on his. 'Look— I'm sorry. I'll get a taxi, you stay here——'

'I wouldn't dream of it.'

'But you'd like a flutter on roulette, wouldn't you?'

'Yes, sure, but——'

She started to stand up. 'Then you shall. That man at the door will get me——' Someone had come up behind her, and she half turned, stiffened when she knew who it was, and heard Jerry say:

'Elena wants to leave. She's very tired——'

'I'm going to get a taxi,' she cut in. 'I don't want to spoil your evening, and I know Jerry would like a game of——'

'Shucks, I can play another night.' Jerry stood up and grinned at her, and Gregor said, very quietly:

'But if you insist, let me take you home.' He looked at Jerry. 'You go and have your game and I shall return in fifteen minutes, no more.'

'Well——' There was a battle going on inside Jerry—and Elena couldn't watch it.

'Thanks, Mr Vlados,' she said. 'It's very kind of you. Although I can quite easily get a taxi——'

'I wouldn't hear of it,' he said, and took her arm.

A few minutes later she was seated in the car. She was seething, and she held her hands clasped tightly on her lap, and she hated everybody. She hadn't felt so unhappy or confused for a long time.

Gregor didn't speak. He drove away from the club, along the dimly lit road and into San Cristobál at a fair speed, slowing down slightly as they left the town behind and the road narrowed. There was no traffic at all, and a high white moon was the only illumination save for the sweeping headlamps of the silent vehicle.

In a minute Elena would be home. It was lonely here. She hadn't thought of that when she decided to come. And Gregor was her only neighbour for miles. Apart from the Bonitas, sleeping soundly in their cottage, she would be alone in the house.

The car slowed, stopped, and they were overlooking the sea, with the moon reflected in a wide white path that shimmered and broke with the movement of the waves, and she looked at him, puzzled.

'We're not there yet,' she said. 'Why have we stopped?'

'Because I wish to talk to you,' he said. Her heart began to bump in fear. Dear God, what had Jerry said? Had he given the game away? Not yet—he mustn't know yet.

'No. I don't want—I'm tired—and you said you'd be back in fifteen——'

'He won't notice. Once he touches those chips he'll forget all about time.'

She shivered. 'Why have you stopped here?'

'Because it is quiet, it is dark—and we are alone.'

'We can talk at the house——'

'And you could run away from me, I think. Here you cannot.'

My God, she thought, what's he going to do? Rape me? She was strong, but she didn't even need to look at him to know he was infinitely stronger. Her tongue stuck to the roof of her mouth with fear, and a tremor ran through her body. This man was dangerous. She had known that ten years ago, and he was stronger, more mature, more dangerous now. Dangerous to her. She knew it instinctively, but there was no way to put it into words.

'Why do you hate me?' he asked softly. It was not what she had expected, yet it was a fact.

'What makes you think—'

'I can see. I am not blind.' He moved his hand, because she had turned away, and he put it on her chin and made her face him. She put her hand up to remove his.

'Take your—your hand away——' her voice was faint.

'When you have answered me I will.'

'You're hurting me!'

'I'm not. I am being very careful not to hurt you. Do you think I would?'

'Yes.'

'Then you are mistaken. I am not a violent man —I am especially not violent with women.'

'You don't need to be—they fawn over you——' She regretted it as she said it, and he laughed softly.

'And does that make you jealous?'

'Don't be stupid—I——'

'I have seen you. You watch me, all the time you watch me. Why?'

'Because I'm going to use you in a book, that's why,' she snapped. 'Now let me *go*!'

'That does not answer my original question.'

'And I don't intend to answer it—and if you want to keep me here all night, go ahead. You don't frighten me.' Which was a lie, but she said it with all the conviction she could. He moved again, softly, swiftly, and not in any way she expected.

He kissed her. It was like no kiss she had ever known before. It was gentle, sensuous; it was the kiss of a virile man who knew how to kiss, to arouse the senses, to devastate and weaken her. His arms moved around her, slowly. She was not aware of that, only on the furthermost edge of her awareness, but it was right, it was part of it, and she was blindingly, dizzyingly aware that she was floating, lost, completely and utterly bound up in a once-in-a-lifetime experience that would—could—last for ever.

Only it didn't. Then it was over, and Gregor drew away from her and said: 'I wondered.' The words lingered in the air, but she was too shaken, too moved to hear them properly, only that they had been said, and nothing would be the same, ever again. She looked ahead blindly, wondering how she could go on here, how she could ever write again. After this. What could she ever write that would match what had just happened? Life had changed, in the timeless instant that the kiss had lasted.

And that was all it had been—a kiss. A wondering, an asking on his part—what would she be like to kiss. He knew now. Elena was fast recovering. The spell was broken.

She turned to face him. 'Take me home,' she said.

His face was shadowed in the dim light from the moon. 'Say please,' he answered, faintly mocking, taunting.

'Please.' It hurt to say it. It physically hurt, but she managed. He reached out to switch on the engine, and he laughed softly, once.

If he had not laughed, if—but he had, and, tormented, Elena reached up to his face, to hurt him—and he caught her hands and held them so that she was powerless. 'Ah no,' he whispered, 'I think not. Do not try to pit your strength against me. You understand?'

The muscles in her arms ached with the silent, desperate struggle and she was breathing rapidly. 'Let me go. Let me go!'

He did so with a suddenness that caught her off balance and Elena, who had had more than enough, reached out, opened her door, stepped out, slammed it shut and began walking down the road towards the trees that hid both their houses. She heard the engine start up and felt an empty sensation at the thought that in a moment she would be alone. At least the house was near. How near? Two—three minutes' walk, that was all. The car purred up, passed her, and was gone, turning right into Gregor's drive and vanishing. Perhaps he'd forgotten that Jerry would be waiting, or perhaps he'd had enough of writers and publishers for one night. Jerry was a big boy, he'd cope. Elena began to whistle softly to chase away the shadows that surrounded her. God, it was dark, and it was silent, and there was no sound, no sign of the car. She wasn't frightened, yet—

She stumbled, turning her ankle on a stone, and hopped for a few steps, wincing. 'Damn, damn!' she muttered. And damn him. She reached her gate and hobbled in, leaning on the gatepost for a moment as she massaged her aching ankle—and realised she had left her handbag, with her key in it, on the seat of Gregor's car. She closed her eyes. What did she do now? March up to his front door and demand it?

'Did you lose anything?' The deep voice came out of the shadows and she nearly overbalanced with the shock. She clutched the gatepost, heart thudding.

'Where—where are you?' she croaked.

'Waiting for you.' He walked forward, holding up her bag. The sense of relief was overwhelming. Elena slipped on her sandal and limped towards him.

'Thank you,' she said with dignity.

'Have you hurt your ankle?'

'No, I always walk like this,' she snapped. 'May I have my bag—*please*?'

'When we reach the house.'

'Why don't you go back to your friends, and Jerry?' she demanded. 'I'm sure they must all be missing you back at the club.'

'Because I said I would bring you home, and I intend to do so.' He walked beside her, glancing occasionally at her foot. 'Did you fall?'

'I tripped over a stone, if you must know,' she gritted. 'Oh, damn!' this as the already precarious heel of her sandal snapped and it brought her foot down with a jolt.

He gave an exclamation that might have been a swearword, or perhaps merely a sound of exasperation, bent down, and scooped her up in his arms before striding off along the drive.

'What are you doing?' she shrilled. 'Put me *down* at——'

'Be quiet!' he thundered in her ear. 'Be *quiet*, or I promise I shall drop you in my swimming pool.'

'You wouldn't dare——'

'Don't dare me.' His voice was harsh. 'You have tried my patience far enough.' She was silent, because he meant what he said, and she was too tired, confused and unhappy to take much more.

He reached the door and handed her the bag after putting her down. 'Open the door.' Elena did so and pushed it open. Gregor followed her and switched on the light, slamming the door shut behind him. She took off her sandals and lifted her skirt slightly, grimacing at her swollen ankle. 'Go and sit down,' he said, as if suddenly weary.

'I can——'

'Go and sit!' He turned on her, eyes bleaker, harder than anything she had seen before.

'I'm not your *dog*!' she stormed, and flung her sandals at him.

'I know. He is a damned sight more obedient than you ever will be!' he grated, and swung her round, pushed her into the lounge and on to a chair. 'Now stay there!' He stood over her, threatening, powerful, and he was angry. Elena shrank back against the cushions, all her fight gone. She had never seen anyone so angry before. She sat very still as he went out, to return moments later with a bowl of cold water. 'Put your foot in that and stay there,' he said.

She did so, and heard the door close, then silence.

Rebelliously, mulishly, she took her foot out and inspected the ankle, wincing as she touched it. Oh, it hurt! And it wouldn't have happened if she hadn't made the grand—and futile—gesture of stalking off alone in the dark, proud and independent.

She heard the door open and hastily dropped her foot back in the water, splashing the delicate silk of her dress as she did so.

Gregor knelt before her, putting down a box on the floor, moved the bowl to one side, opened the box, which had bandages and creams in, and said: 'I'm going to put something on your foot to ease it. Before I start do you want to fight about it?' He glanced up briefly as he said it, and Elena shook her head. 'Good.'

He unrolled a crêpe bandage and she watched him. She could see only the top of his head and his shoulders and arms clearly. His hair grew thick and straight, jet black, gleaming under the light, his shoulders were broad and his arms were muscular. He had rolled up his shirt sleeves to the elbows, and his forearms were covered in dark hair and immensely powerful-looking. Yet his hands were gentle. They were as gentle as any doctor's, and she felt no pain from his touch. Her breath caught in her throat and a warmth filled her, a treacherous betraying warmth. She had never wanted a man before. Men—many men—had desired her, but she had never given herself to any. She was cool, unapproachable, and it had always been—so far, no further. But she wanted Gregor to make love to her. The sensation was overwhelming and frightening and infinitely disturbing. Because she hated him at the same time her body betrayed her.

'Did I hurt you?' She must have made a sound—a sound of pain—but not what he imagined.

'No, it was—nothing.' The job was done. She had a neatly strapped up ankle and he had applied some cream that was cooling and very soothing, and she felt much better. 'Thank you.'

He straightened, and glanced down at her. 'Stand up. See how you walk now.' Barefoot Elena walked to the door. It hurt, of course, but not as much. She could walk, that was the main thing. She couldn't meet his eyes. She was frightened of what hers might show.

'Yes, that's fine. Thank you.'

'You have no need to keep thanking me,' he replied. 'I will clear away, and then go back for your—Jerry.'

'And I'll go to bed.'

'That is why you left, isn't it? Because you were so tired?' Was there a trace of mockery there? She bit her lip.

'I've been travelling for hours,' she answered.

'Of course. And tomorrow you will be writing.'

'Yes.' She could at last meet his eyes. They were disconcertingly dark and shadowed—and unreadable. What went on in his mind? 'I have a lot of work to do.'

'Did you see any books of mine that would help

you?' he asked.

'I didn't have time,' she answered.

'Then you must come over any time you wish.'

'That's very kind of you. I'll remember that.' She wished he would go. She wanted to think about what had happened to her, about her own treacherous weakness. She wanted to scream at him, tell him to get out—but she stood there calmly instead, because if she did that, she would be giving herself away, and he would know. He must never know. She had seen the way women behaved with him, the simpering, the fluttering, and he expected it—he probably enjoyed it.

'And was it true what you said in the car?'

She had forgotten what she had said in that car, except that she had very probably made a complete fool of herself. She searched her brains, and he added helpfully: 'That you were using me in a book?'

'Oh, *that*!' She tried to laugh, but it didn't quite come off. 'Why don't you wait and see?'

'I suppose I must be flattered if so,' he said, and he was watching her, like a cat watches a mouse; he was playing a little game with her and she certainly didn't know what it was, but she didn't like it.

'Why don't you go and fetch Jerry?' she said. 'It must be an hour now—he'll be wondering——' she stopped.

'Wondering what? Do you always change the subject when you don't wish to answer?'

'I wasn't aware I had,' she retorted. 'You'd re-marked that you must be flattered. It wasn't a question, was it?'

'It was originally. You didn't answer that. You told me to wait and see.'

'That *was* my answer.' She leaned against a chair back to rest her foot.

'And what might Jerry be wondering? Do you think he will consider you unsafe with me?'

'Of course not! I——'

'He loves you?'

'It's none of your business!'

He smiled, slowly. 'Of course not. But I ask it anyway. I would say yes, to judge by the way he looks at you——'

'Then you didn't need to ask, did you?' she re-torted. 'Are *you* in love with anyone?'

'No.' But still the cynical smile touched his lips with mockery. Why had she asked such a stupid question? She didn't know. 'I have never met one that——' he shrugged carelessly, 'I would want to love enough to spend my life with.'

'But you can play the field, can't you? You wouldn't need to marry——' she was horrified at herself, even as the words came out. She knew her eyes were wide with her own dismay. She wanted to bite her tongue, to stop herself.

'Do you mean—do I have affairs? Mistresses?'

It was precisely what she had meant—but she would die before admitting it. 'Perhaps you had better go,' she said stiffly. 'I don't think——'

'Are you frightened?'

'Of course not. I just don't like the turn this conversation is taking. I——'

'But you started it.'

'I didn't!' she denied. Had she? She couldn't remember now. Her head was muzzy with tiredness, and with all that had happened.

'It was perhaps all in the cause of research?' he suggested in deceptively gentle tones. 'You must know all about your characters before you use them, no?'

'Not necessarily. I can make up——'

'And you do it so well. I have read two of your books. They are very good. They are also very descriptive——' he paused, and smiled. Elena's heart was bumping. That was the last thing she had expected to hear. *He* had read two of her books. Somehow she never visualised her readers; they were mostly women anyway.

She said, with great dignity, she thought: 'You're very kind. I wouldn't have expected you to have heard of me. And I certainly wouldn't have expected you to read what are essentially women's books.'

'Not usually, I admit. But then I knew you were coming here, so I made a point of it. In case I ever met you,' he added softly. And somehow there was more in those last few words than was on the surface. They said more. She didn't know what it was, but it scared her, as other, little things had done. Things now forgotten, but disturbing in a vague way at the time.

'When—when did you know I was coming here?' she had to know.

'It was in all the island's newspapers a week or so ago—didn't *you* know? And a photograph or two. They did not do you justice. You are far more beautiful than they showed.'

The trouble was, he didn't make it sound like a compliment, not like Jerry would have done, or any other men. He made it sound quite coldly clinical, as though he was assessing a painting.

'Thank you. Perhaps we can talk about my writing another time. I really am very tired, and I'm sure Jerry will be wondering where you are. After all, he wants to talk about *your* writing, doesn't he?'

'We talked enough.'

'Oh, I know you did. That's why I went to have a shower. I realised you wanted to talk. The only trouble is you didn't seem to be talking writing when I returned.'

He smiled. 'He was telling me some American jokes.'

'I can imagine,' she said frostily. She looked pointedly at the bowl, and at his first aid box on the floor.

'You make yourself very clear,' he said softly, and went to pick them both up. 'Why do you not just tell me to go?'

'I've been trying to do that for the last ten minutes,' she retorted. 'But you're impervious to hints—or has no one told you?'

He laughed as he went out. She hated him laughing at her. She didn't know why, but she did. She followed him to the kitchen, saw him empty the bowl. 'I shall leave the box here until tomorrow,' he said. 'Do you know you have a burglar alarm?'

'What?' The quick change of subject took her by surprise.

'A burglar alarm.' He repeated it slowly, as though to a child, and she felt herself flush.

'No, I didn't. Where is it?'

'Here.' He opened a cupboard and pointed to a box inside. 'I found it when I came out for the bowl.' He opened the box and twisted a key. 'That is now on. Understand?'

'Yes.'

'Good.' He switched it off. 'Now, when I am gone —and yes, I *am* leaving now, turn it on again. I will certainly hear it from my house. If it ever goes off, I will know you need me.'

Then—and then, for the first time, Elena realised something she should have realised straight away, when she had first discovered they were next door neighbours in fact. And she stood very still, absolutely rigid with horror, and white-faced. *He must have known Uncle Jim.* And if he knew Uncle, he would know who she was.

The room swayed and blurred, and he caught her. 'My God, Elena, what is it?'

She couldn't tell him. She couldn't even speak.

She felt his arms around her, those traitor's arms. He knew—he *must* know. She wanted to escape, but where to?

'I—I——' she gasped.

'Ssh, don't try to talk. I will carry you upstairs. You must lie down.' Gregor picked her up as though she was light as a feather, and carried her up the stairs to her room. Then he laid her on the bed. 'I will go and get you some water,' he said, went over to the washbowl and rinsed out the glass there, and filled it.

Elena had to know the worst before he left. She sipped the cool water and lay back. 'I'm very silly,' she said. 'I've just realised I'd not eaten since lunch.' It was true, but it wasn't the reason for her apparent faint. It was an adequate excuse, however. 'I'll be better in a moment, then I'll get myself something to eat.'

'Let me. Is there food in the refrigerator?'

'Yes, Jerry had it stocked up. There's tinned soup as well——'

'Then I will get you some.' Gregor went out. How did she ask? She prepared the casual question, rehearsed it, and when he returned with the soup she asked, as she spooned it up: 'Have you lived in your present house for a while?' She already knew the answer to that. It was almost exactly ten years.

'Not very long, why?' The answer surprised her, but she could hardly tell him she knew he was lying.

'I wondered. The old man I bought this house from——' now was the danger point, if he knew——then she would know too, immediately. 'I wondered if you were close neighbours, that's all—if you'd been in here before.' That was a nice, innocent touch, an afterthought.

'Ah, I see. I work many hours. And he was virtually a recluse, you know—or of course, you didn't know.' He smiled. 'Is the soup making you feel better?'

'Yes, I'm fine.' She was too. The danger point had passed and the sense of relief was overwhelming.

'Then I will go. Sleep—don't forget to switch on the alarm when I have left.'

'I will. Goodnight.' She smiled at him, in relief more than anything, but he wouldn't know that. The next minute she was alone, and she heard him close the door, and the lock catching, and she could relax.

But not for long. She awoke from disturbing dreams of Gregor and sat up in bed, perspiration pouring off her, gasping with fear. He was laughing, long low mocking laughter that had filled her mind, echoing and re-echoing, because he knew exactly who she was, and why she had come, and he knew everything about her.

It took her a long time to get to sleep after that.

CHAPTER FOUR

THE hammering on the door woke her the second time, and Elena pulled on her dressing gown and went downstairs, yawning, hair tousled with sleep, wondering who on earth was calling at this unearthly hour of the—she saw the clock in the hall. It was half past ten.

Jerry nearly fell in when she opened the door and immediately a clangour of bells filled the house, deafening them. 'Oh, my God!' he groaned, holding his head.

'The alarm! Hang on.' She switched it off and went back to where he stood swaying gently in the hall. He looked as though he were suffering from a hangover—and more than that, he didn't look very pleased with her. That makes two of us, she thought. I'm not terribly pleased with *you*.

'Coffee?' she asked.

'Black, please.' He followed her into the kitchen and sat down. 'I'm catching a plane in two hours—but I had to come and see you first.'

'That was nice of you. You remembered me, did you?'

Jerry squinted owlishly up at her from his seat. 'I'm the one making the funnies, not you,' he said. 'What the hell were you doing with him all that time?'

'Oh, didn't he tell you? I sprained my ankle.'

'Yes, he told me. Something about you getting out for a walk and tripping.'

'That's about it.' She handed him his cup. 'One coffee, hot and black.'

'Listen, Elena, you went off in a huff——'

'You could say that. You were supposed to be looking after me, taking me out, remember?' She gave him a level glance. 'And I also seem to remember you saying you didn't fancy him as my neighbour. It didn't stop you letting me go home with him, did it?'

He groaned again. 'Don't shout—I'm delicate.'

'You look hung over to me. I suppose you drank too much.'

He looked sheepish. 'Well——'

'Oh, don't bother, I'm not your wife.' Elena sipped her own coffee. 'Want any toast?'

'No, thanks. Listen, honey, I'm sorry. Perhaps I was wrong, staying on like that—but I was just so caught up in it all. I knew you'd be safe with Vlados.'

'You knew?' she raised her eyebrows. 'After what you've just said? It doesn't sound like it——'

'Yes, well, I didn't expect him to be two hours, did I? But when he explained——'

'Oh, so *he* explained. You just wanted to hear my side as well, did you? To see if they tallied? *Thanks!*'

'God, you're sharp this morning. I'd better go——'

'I told you writers were difficult. I haven't even begun. Fine publisher you are, ditching me just because he's written a couple of chapters of his life story. Hah! I thought you hated them.'

'I hadn't seen this, though, had I? That is different. Boy, is it different!'

'And business comes first. Yes, I see that now. And yes, you'd better go, because I'm a writer, and *my writing* comes first with me.' She was wiping the floor with him, and she had never done it before, and she didn't know why she was doing it now, except that somewhere Gregor Vlados was at the bottom of it. He usually was.

Then as if on cue, he walked in. Elena looked up and glared at him, and Jerry looked up as if someone had come to rescue him, and grinned and said: 'Am I glad to see you! I'm getting a rocket from Elena——'

'I heard the alarm. I was in a shower——' Gregor looked at them both.

'I opened the door. I forgot,' she said. She waited for him to leave, and perhaps she made it too obvious, for he pulled out a chair and sat down opposite Jerry at the table.

'Would you like a coffee? Now you're here,' she said sweetly, acidly.

'Why, thank you. Black, please.'

'Don't tell me you drank too much as well?'

'No, I drink very little. I just prefer black coffee.' Gregor gave her a kind gentle smile in return. The subtle undercurrents she had noticed before were suddenly in the room. Only Jerry remained impervious. He sipped his coffee solemnly, and looked as though he would prefer to be lying down in a darkened room rather than flying on a plane. Elena felt a pang of sympathy. She was blaming him for something he couldn't help.

Gregor waited until she had handed him the coffee, thanked her, then said: 'I am sorry. Have I interrupted your talk?'

'Hell no, stay,' begged Jerry. 'It's not a talk, more a lecture——'

'I'm sure Mr Vlados doesn't want to hear——'

'Please, call me Gregor,' he cut in. 'And now I am here, perhaps I could run you to the airport? Unless,' this with a delicately enquiring glance at Elena, 'you are taking him?'

'I'd better not drive today, with my sprained ankle,' she answered.

'Of course! Forgive me. How is it?'

'Nearly better, thanks to your expert bandaging.'

'I'll look at it later for you if you like. I'm not a doctor, but I have a fair knowledge of first aid.'

'That's kind of you, but I wouldn't put you to the trouble——'

'It is no trouble. It's the least I can do, for a neighbour.'

She wanted to hit him, scream, and run. It was the strangest thing that had ever happened to her. They were there; on the surface the conversation was perfectly normal, and yet underneath, swirling undercurrents made her feel breathless and afraid.

Yet Jerry was totally unaware of anything. It's as though, she thought, with blinding insight, we could have a blazing row, just by a word, an inflection, a gesture—and no one else would know. And only he and I know. That was the oddest thing of all: he *knew*.

He smiled now at her, as if he was letting her know he read her every thought. 'I shall not go to work today. I too shall stay at home and write.'

'How nice,' she murmured. She turned and went over to the cooker and switched on the grill, and Jerry said:

'That's great, Gregor. And Elena will be on hand to give you any tips, won't you, honey?'

She could have killed him there and then. He got up, stumbling slightly. 'Say, honey, where's the bathroom?'

'There's one by the front door. Mind the two steps down,' she answered. Then he had gone, and she knew, by the prickle at the back of her neck, that Gregor was behind her. His body didn't touch hers, but she could feel it as though it did.

'Will you?' he whispered.

She didn't answer; she was concentrating on breathing instead. His hand encircled her wrist. 'I said—will you?' he repeated softly.

'Go to hell!' The words shuddered out of her, and he laughed softly, satisfied. Then he moved away and she put two slices of bread under the grill with hands that shook uncontrollably.

Jerry decided after all that he would have toast,

so she made more, and watched them both eat it, then Gregor looked at his watch and said: 'If you are to catch your plane it might be sensible to move soon.'

'Yep, you're right.' Jerry smiled winningly at her. 'Hurry up and get dressed.'

'But I'm not——' Then she saw Gregor's face. Of course he expected her not to go, that was why he had offered to run Jerry in the first place. 'All right,' she said. 'It'll only take me ten minutes.' She drifted out, the long pale gold negligee swirling after her. Jerry was going to get a most surprisingly affectionate goodbye kiss.

Elena showered, chose a low-necked blue sundress that set off her figure to perfection, studied herself briefly in the mirror, satisfied, put on her most expensive and favourite perfume, 'Joy', and combed her dark hair, then a swift smoothing of lipstick, and she was ready. The perfection was marred only slightly by the neat but obvious bandage, but that couldn't be helped. She put on a pair of flat-heeled white sandals, picked up her bag, and went downstairs.

'I'm ready,' she announced.

Gregor stood up. 'I will bring my car round,' he said. 'One moment.'

'Hadn't you better give me the keys of the hire car?' Elena suggested. 'If I'm to be using it?'

'Of course. Sorry, honey, I forgot.' He looked up at her. 'Now he's gone, and before he gets back—say you're not angry with me?'

'I'm not. I'm sorry I snapped, but——'

'It's okay, you don't need to explain. I behaved badly. I won't do it again, and I'll be here at the weekend to make up for it.'

'And we'll have a lovely time.' She intended it to be so. She timed her next words carefully. She waited until she heard the brief tap at the front door, and Gregor's footsteps in the hall, then said to Jerry: 'Look, it's rather silly to stay at an hotel when you come again. There's plenty of room here.' Gregor had heard. She had intended him to.

'Really?' Jerry's eyes lit up. Down, boy, she thought. There is absolutely no need for you to get any ideas at all.

'Of course. Then you and—Gregor can talk all you want. In between us going out, of course, and me writing.' She smiled sweetly at the waiting man. His face was devoid of any expression, it was a studied blandness.

'My cases are in the hire car, I'll get them.' Jerry went ahead, whistling softly, and Elena laughed.

'Shall I switch on the alarm? Oh, no, better not, the housekeeper might arrive. Are we ready?' She swept a glance round the kitchen for anything left switched on. 'Everything off. Let's go.' She sailed out, and Gregor followed.

Negra was sitting in the car, tail wagging, as Jerry transferred his case to the boot of the Rolls. 'I'll sit in the back with him, you men can sit in front,' said Elena, and did so.

Gregor drove off, slowly down the drive, then faster along the road, through the town, and past the night club to the airport. He and Jerry talked, and she stroked the dog who was resting his head on her knee. When she got back to the house she really must try and write. She had put the kiss of Gregor's firmly to the back of her mind, where it belonged. How stupid she had been to have made such a fuss of a kiss! She had acted like a starstruck teenager. They meant nothing. His certainly meant less than nothing. Less than nothing.

They had a half-hour delay at the airport, and had a coffee in the departure lounge, and there were no undercurrents at all. Gregor was charming, and Jerry responded. Again, it seemed as if everyone knew Gregor. They had had instant attention, were seated in a quiet comfortable corner, and he constantly acknowledged greetings from passing staff and passengers. Elena was the only one who wasn't charmed by him, but she hid it well, and when it was time for Jerry to go, hugged him warmly and gave him a lovely kiss. The men shook hands, a white-jacketed porter appeared as if by magic to take his luggage, and they stood by the window to see him get on the plane.

Then the tension came back. As she stood by Gregor's side, Elena could feel herself tightening, could feel the tingle at the back of her neck that always gave her warning when he was too near.

'There he is,' he said softly, and she looked, waved to the small figure who was waving to them, watched him walk up the ramp, and on to the plane.

'Well, that's it,' she said. 'Shall we go?'

'Of course.' She moved away before he could take her arm, and led the way out to the car. He opened the front passenger door and she slid in and greeted Negra, who whined as if they had been away for a day instead of half an hour.

When Gregor drove out of the airfield he turned left instead of right. 'But this is the wrong——' she began.

'I know. I thought I would take you a little ride round the island—after all, this is your first visit, isn't it?'

'Yes.'

'Then you must see the beauty spots, and you will be able to show them to Jerry when he comes again at weekend. Is he a very busy man?'

'Very.'

'And successful?'

'Of course. Are you afraid he'll rob you over your books?'

'No. I was thinking how flattered you should be having him spending so much time with you when he clearly leads a very full life.'

'He makes the time,' she responded sweetly. They were slowing now, and she knew where they were going. The cliffs to the right of them had a concealed path down to the beach and some caves, but she wasn't supposed to know that. He stopped the car and they got out, Negra bounding off delightedly to sniff at some bushes, and Gregor looked down at her. Elena wished now that she hadn't worn flat sandals. He towered over her, and she felt absurdly small, like a child. 'Where are we going?' she asked.

'Come, I will show you.' He called the dog, who ran back, tongue lolling out, almost seeming to smile. 'You might have to take my hand. Will that bother you?'

'Why?' She knew, of course. The path down was steep and narrow—not dangerous, but not to be taken recklessly.

'Because we are going down there,' he pointed, and the view was dizzying from that height, 'and because you have hurt your ankle.'

'Then it seems sensible.'

'Good.' He held out his left hand, and she took it. His clasp was warm and firm, and the warmth of him tingled up her arm. Negra led the way and they followed slowly and steadily. There were handholds at either side. The path had been literally carved out of solid rock, and it was layered almost like shallow steps—but Gregor's hand was more steady and sure than anything Elena had ever wanted and she knew then what she should have known all along, ever since she had seen him at his hotel. She stopped, frightened, and he stopped too.

'What is it?'

'I just want to——' her voice was shaky, 'look at the view.'

'Then we shall.' Negra had reached the sand, and sat waiting for them patiently. They were half way down. The sheer cliff face was at the back of them, in front the sea, and the rocks, stretching away, the sea hazy at the horizon, the sky cloudless, a deep azure blue with a high sun to dazzle. It was very hot.

'Mmm, beautiful,' she said, but her heart bumped crazily because of the dreadful, treacherous thing she now knew. When Gregor had taken her hand, she knew. When he had kissed her the previous night, she hadn't been sure, and had tried to resist it. But it was too late now. Ten years too late.

He led the way again, and she, less surefooted, followed so that his pace was slower to accommodate her. Then the last leap down, and he took it, turned, and caught and lifted her down, putting her on the sand gently.

'We are here. Let us sit. In a minute we will go and see the caves.' He lay down and stretched himself luxuriously. 'Ah!'

Elena sat down a few feet away. She was still rather shattered. She wished she were alone. She watched the water, dazzling with sunlight on it, watched the foamy breakers shush to a murmur and disappear into the golden sand near them. It was beautiful here, it was truly beautiful. She had been here with her parents and brother when she was a child, and she remembered the two occasions clearly. They had picnicked on the beach, and swum in the sea, and explored the caves. And if this man had not appeared, they might still be living on Cristobál. She might be here with them now, instead of him ... She wanted to weep, for the sadness and waste of it all. She should tell him now, should tell him why she was here—then it would all be over. She need never see him again. She could write her book, sell the house, and leave. And never return. For all her plans for revenge had crumbled like dust; she knew it as surely as she knew that she was in love with him.

She turned her head to see him, and he was asleep. Helpless, knowing she shouldn't, she looked at him, searching the cool hard planes of his face, seeking hungrily, storing every detail in her mind for the time when she would no longer be here and this memory would be all she would have of him. His mouth was gentle in sleep, not hard nor cruel, but almost tender. She wanted to touch his face, to stroke the curve from cheekbone to jaw, to touch, sensually, and know the tingle in her blood that he roused in her by his nearness, but she sat very still and looked instead.

Then he opened his eyes and they were upon her. Confused, she stammered: 'I wondered how long you would sleep.'

'I wasn't. I was thinking I would like to go swimming,' he answered.

'Here?'

He laughed. 'The water is here. Where else?'

If it was a pass, it was a crude one. She thought he would have been more subtle than that. 'I sup-

pose the next thing you say is, what a shame we've
no swimsuits—I've heard it before.'

His mouth curved into a smile. 'You think that is
my way? You are mistaken. I am wearing swimming trunks underneath—by chance, not intention.
I was showering after swimming in my pool this
morning when I heard your alarm sound. I grabbed
my trunks and put them on again——'

'There's a coincidence,' she murmured. 'And
what about me?'

Gregor shrugged. 'I said *I* would like to swim.
Have I suggested you should?'

'Not yet, but you will I'm sure.'

'Do you want to?'

She was silent. Of course I want to, dammit, she
wanted to say.

'No,' she answered shortly.

'Do you mind if I do?'

'I don't care what you do.' She lay back as if that
closed the subject. She heard him move, heard the
chink of his belt, and she kept her eyes closed.
When she opened them both he and the dog were
in the sea. Elena stood up. The hell with it, she
thought. She was boiling, her bra and pants were
flowered cotton, practically indistinguishable from
a bikini—and she felt reckless. She peeled off her
dress, kicked off her sandals, then, remembering,
put her contact lenses safely in their container in
her bag, and walked into the water. Everything was
a glorious blur in the distance. Near to, she could
see two heads in the water, not terribly clear, but

clear enough. She leaned into the waves and struck out towards them.

He laughed. 'You changed your mind?'

'Yes. And I'm quite respectable.'

'I know, I watched you. Do you have to take your —er—lenses out?'

'Yes. I might lose them.' It was heavenly in the warm water. It was balm to the skin, soothing. She turned and swam lazily away from him, turned on her back, and floated, eyes closed. She thought about him and how she had hated him. It was odd, but in a way she still did, for what he had done to her mother and father. That was in one part of her, her mind, the logical part. But the heart knows no logic, it is not governed by the same rules. Perhaps it wasn't even that, but physical, an infatuation—the blinding desire for an experienced virile man. Perhaps, if we had an affair, I might be cured, she thought, and shivered, frightened. When she gave herself to a man, it would be for one reason only, because she loved him with all her heart and mind. It wasn't love she felt for Gregor, it couldn't be—not while she could never forgive what he had done. Oh God, she thought, help me, I'm so mixed up. She turned and began swimming again, the tears and salt water blinding her so that everything was a gold misty blur. Then she collided with a hard body, heard him say: 'Careful—you're not looking where you're——' then he stopped and caught hold of her, and guided her into the shallows, where they found their feet and stood up.

'Why,' he said, 'what is it?'

Elena blinked, looked away. 'Nothing. The salt water irritates my eyes.'

.'Why are you crying?'

'I told you, it's——'

'No, it is not. Look at me.'

She pushed him away and began to walk out, but he followed, and caught her. 'Leave me *alone*!' she cried. But he was much bigger and stronger, and now, again, his very nearness was a disturbing threat to her reason. His arms were gripping hers and he forced her to face him, and she saw his eyelashes, spiky wet, and his dripping hair, and his tanned face and body, and she caught her breath, helpless, dizzy, suddenly intensely aware of him, so aware that she could not move away. And as he kissed her, slowly, fiercely, she put her arms around his body and clung to him.

She felt the hard sand beneath her, the water lapping round them, Gregor's body upon hers, and she was lost, lost in the timeless wonder of what was happening, of what she had known would happen all along, because this, now, was all she had ever wanted. His hands caressed her subtly, sensuously, under the water, his mouth found her again, and the hard length of him was against her, a fiery caress independent of his hands. She moaned softly and pulled his head closer, heard him murmur: 'Dear God, I want you now,' and thought, only half consciously, with the tiny fraction of her logical mind that was functioning—now, now—but I shouldn't, it's wrong, it was here, ten years ago—the thought disappeared as a wave rippled up and covered their bodies, cooling the heat, but not putting out the fire.

Then Negra, sensing perhaps a game to which he hadn't been invited, took a flying leap out of the water, and barking happily, landed squarely beside them, sending up a shower of sand and salt water over them. Gregor said something very violently in Russian, and the spell which had transformed her was broken. Elena sat up, dazed, pulled herself from under him and scrambled to her feet, sobbing and gasping for breath.

She ran to where her dress lay, scrabbling for it, sensed Gregor behind her, then he caught and pulled her up. 'Elena——' he said harshly.

'Let me go!' She was panicking, and caught him on the chest with her elbow. There was the taste of blood in her mouth, and she touched the cut on her lip with trembling fingers. He had bitten her. 'Don't touch me,' she gasped. 'Leave me——' she struggled, but he was too strong for her. She felt her own strength ebbing as he pulled her towards him, and he was like a man in a trance, and she was frightened. He was going to rape her ...

She pulled his hair hard, jerking his head to one side, and hit him in the face. The spell was broken for him too. He stood back, panting, dark-faced, bitter, and spat out: 'Don't worry, I won't touch you again.' He turned and began to put on his trousers, and after a moment's trembling indecision, Elena picked up her dress and slipped it over her head. Then, very quietly, she sat down on the sand and put her face in her hands.

'Are you ready to leave?'

She shook her head. 'Leave me here.' She didn't want to go anywhere with him.

'Don't be stupid!' His voice was harsh, and he pulled her to her feet. 'Get your purse. We are leaving now. You are quite safe with me—now.' His mouth twisted into a smile that was not pleasant. 'I have no desire to touch you ever again.'

She faced him defiantly. 'Is that what you brought me here for? To make love to me? I'm sorry to disappoint you.' Her mouth trembled. She could still taste the blood.

'No. You know that—it—happened——'

'I don't believe you!' Her eyes glistened with bright tears.

'Would I have brought the dog if so?' He was toweringly angry, he was rigid with anger, but it was controlled—the more potentially explosive for that. 'You were weeping—you were upset——'

'And you wanted to comfort me. Is that how you do it?' Her voice was a mere whisper. Her anger was partly for herself, but he couldn't know that. She lifted her chin defiantly. 'I must remember not to—to cry——' she stopped, unable to go on.

Gregor closed his eyes. 'We had better go. I am not leaving you here, you are too many miles from home.' He picked up her handbag and gave it to

her. 'I shall not offer my assistance climbing up—
you might misunderstand it. Go first.'

She fumbled for her contact lenses, found them,
turned away and put them in. Then she set off
walking to the cliff path.

They drove home in silence, and Gregor left her
at her front door and went away. She went in,
locked the door and ran upstairs to change. That
was it. She would not see him again.

CHAPTER FIVE

THE housekeeper had been in and cleaned the house. The kitchen was sparklingly clean, and there was a little vase of fresh flowers on the window-sill. Elena touched them gently. If she wasn't to brood, she might as well research and make notes for her book. There was a room next to her bed-room that held a desk, and here she set out her books and paper and pens.

It didn't come easily at first, but gradually she found herself relaxing and the notebook filled satis-fyingly, and she lost all count of time. She looked up because she found it difficult to see and dis-covered to her surprise that it was growing dusk outside. And she was hungry.

She flexed her aching fingers and went down-stairs to switch on a few lights and prepare a meal. She didn't care what she ate, it was merely a ques-tion of filling her empty stomach, so she settled for a cheese sandwich and a cup of coffee, and was about to carry them upstairs to have while she con-tinued when the telephone shrilled, nearly making her drop the cup and plate. 'Damn!' She put them down on a chair and picked up the telephone.

'Hello?' The phone crackled, buzzed, and clicked a few times, then:

'Hello, it's me, Jerry——'

'Did you have a good journey?'

'Fine. Listen, honey—this is one hell of a line, and what a job I've had getting through. Can you get Gregor to the phone, *please*——'

'But can't you phone him yourself?'

'Sure I could, if I knew his number. Do you?'

He had told it her last night, but it had gone completely. 'No—but I'm busy, Jerry, can't it wait——'

'Listen, love, it's taken me half an hour to get through to you—I might not make it and this is *urgent*——'

'But it will cost you a fortune to hold on——'

'I know. So be quick, okay?'

She took a deep breath. 'All right.' She ran out, across the garden, through the gap in the trees, and up the steps. The light shone out from Gregor's room, and the french windows were open, but the room was empty. Negra rose and greeted her warmly, and she ran into the hall and shouted: 'Gregor?'

There was silence for a moment, then his voice came: 'Yes?' It held no welcome, none at all. Elena swallowed.

'Jerry's on the phone—my phone—and wants to speak to you urgently. Can you come now, please?'

Another brief silence, and during it, she thought she heard a woman's voice, low and quiet, then Gregor's voice: 'I'll be down now.'

She turned away puzzled, curious, and heard him running down. He wore dark trousers and white shirt and he looked at her. 'On *your* telephone?'

'Yes. He's phoning from New York.'

He walked past her and went out of the open french windows. She knew she had to go back, but more than anything she wanted to know if she had imagined that woman's voice. There was a small sick feeling inside her as she realised the implications if it were.

She couldn't go up and look, that would be unforgivable. But if she pretended she had heard a noise——

'Hello?' she called. 'Is anyone there?'

Her heartbeats nearly deafened her. She was sure they could be heard a mile away. Then there was a thud, a sound as if of a chair being moved, and a door upstairs softly opened. Then silence, a waiting silence.

Elena's nerve broke, and she fled. Heart in mouth, sickened, she ran through the gardens and through her open french windows, to hear Gregor's voice on the telephone.

'——yes, yes, I understand. I will do it, Jerry, of course—do you want Elena back?'

Apparently not, for he said goodbye then, and hung up. Stiff-faced, she thought she had better make her confession first, and said: 'I thought I heard a noise upstairs at your house. I shouted out, but no one answered.'

There was a momentary pause, then he said: 'It's all right, I know. Do you have a typewriter I may borrow?'

'Yes. Why?' She could scarcely speak.

'Because Jerry wants his editor to see my first chapter as soon as possible, and I must type it tonight and keep a copy in case it gets lost in the post.'

'I see.' She swallowed. 'Can you type?'

'No. But I will manage.'

'In one night?' That was funny. She nearly smiled, only she didn't feel like smiling. She felt like hurting him for what he was doing. She felt sick with a treacherous, torturing jealousy so that she wanted to scream. But she didn't.

'Yes, if necessary.'

'Don't be silly! It's impossible. I—I'll do it.'

'You?' His mouth twisted. 'But you are writing.'

'It can wait one night.' She didn't know why she had offered. He might forgive her for today, if she did.

'Then—thank you.' He nodded imperceptibly, a small mocking bow. 'I shall go and fetch it.'

As he walked out, Elena couldn't help herself, she asked, 'Is it a woman at your house?'

He turned, softly, slowly. 'Yes.'

Her lips were cold. 'I'm—sorry. It's none of my business.'

He smiled. 'You are right, it isn't.' He turned away and walked out.

Sick at heart, Elena went upstairs to bring down her typewriter. For some reason she didn't want to do Gregor's typing in the room she used for her own writing. She took it into the kitchen, laid out paper and carbons, and waited for his return.

He was back in a few minutes and she called out: 'I'm in the kitchen.'

'What time shall I come over for it?' He walked in.

'I'll bring it when I've done. I should have finished by——' she glanced at the ten closely written sheets—— 'about eleven.'

'Then I will come over for it myself. Thank you.' He was grave, courteous, and like a remote stranger.

'As you wish.' She waited for him to go, then put the two sheets and carbon into the typewriter. But before she started the actual typing, she began to read through.

She knew within minutes why Jerry had reacted as he had. She knew it was not only good, it was better than anything she had ever written in her life. It was liquid poetry, it had a force and power, and it was tender and funny and sad. She closed her eyes and laid the sheets down. Dear lord, she thought, has this been written by that man? She put her hand to her mouth, seeing him again in her mind's eye so vividly that it was as if he were there with her in the room. She had not seen tenderness in him. She had seen passion, and fire and anger, and that inherent power—but she had not known that deep down he had a heart and a soul of such caring that it hurt to know. It hurt because he had revealed himself on paper, and she was deeply moved. Yet his words were simple, easily read.

She took a deep breath, went to make herself a

coffee, and then sat down to finish what he had written.

Twenty minutes later she began to type. She typed more slowly and carefully than usual, because she wanted it to be perfect for him. She took a break to rest her aching fingers and stiff back when she was half way through, made herself another coffee, then started again. She was concentrating so deeply, all other thoughts out of her mind, that it was with a sense of shock that she realised someone was standing in the doorway, watching her. She looked up and blinked. It was Gregor—of course.

'I'm nearly——' she looked at her watch. It was past eleven. 'Is it that time?' She was nearly dizzy with tiredness and the effort of concentration. 'I won't be long. Look, sit down and read through while I finish—check I've made no mistakes—I'll not be long, I've only about five more pages to do.'

He sat down quietly and picked up the numbered typewritten pages, and Elena continued typing at a slightly quicker speed. She finished another page and pulled it out, handed it to him.

'Would you make me a drink, please? I'm sorry I'm taking so long, but I wanted it to be just right.'

'Of course. I am grateful. What would you like? Coffee, tea—alcohol?'

She needed a good stiff drink at that moment. 'I've none in,' she said, rolling the papers carefully into the typewriter. 'Tea will do——'

'Shall I go and get you one? What would you like?'

It would get him out of the way for a few minutes. She found it harder to concentrate with him there. 'I'd like a vodka and tonic, please.'

'Very well.' He put the paper down carefully, and went out. Elena began typing. Gregor was back before she had finished the page, carrying two bottles and two tall glasses. He put ice in, filled them up, and handed her a glass. She took a good swallow.

'That's better. Thanks.'

He read silently. She typed on, pausing for an occasional sip of the cool refreshing drink. Then at last it was done. She tore the last sheets out of the typewriter, separated the two copies, and rubbed her aching neck.

'Have you an envelope?' she asked him. 'Because if not, I have some. I'll address it for you to post first thing in the morning.'

'Thank you. Better still, I will post it tonight.'

'I've no stamps.'

'I have. I will fetch them.' He was still the polite, courteous stranger.

She watched him go and went up for an envelope to her study. When he returned she handed him the now typed envelope.

'That's it,' she said. 'Any errors?'

'None. It's perfect.'

'Keep your copy in a safe place. I hope the post is reliable.'

'Reasonably so.' He smiled faintly. 'Thank you for this. I am grateful.'

'Can I go with you to post it?'

'If you wish.' But he looked faintly surprised.

'I need a break, that's all. I've been sitting here typing, and I don't fancy a walk in the dark on my own, so——' she shrugged, 'a ride will clear my head. But you don't have to take me if you don't want to——' she faltered at what she saw in his eyes, and went pink. 'I mean—don't feel you're obliged to take me because I've typed that——'

'I don't. Of course you may come. I was rather surprised because I did not think you would want to, that is all.' His face gave nothing away.

'I'm sorry about today—I behaved badly——'

'Perhaps it is better not mentioned again. I would prefer it, and so, I think, would you.' He folded the typewritten sheets into the envelope and sealed it up, then stuck on two stamps and a blue airmail sticker. 'That is done. Shall we go?'

Elena finished her drink and stood up, picking up her keys from the dresser by the door. 'Shall I bring my car round or will you walk through to my house?'

'I'll walk—I need some exercise.' She closed the door behind her and followed him round in the darkness. The air was cool, and the sky was full of bright diamonds. The moon had been hidden by the trees, but she saw it as she went into his garden, high, pale and bright. They walked round to where the Rolls was parked at the front and he opened the door for her before getting in himself. She sat back enjoying the cool breeze that came in through the open window, closed her eyes and tried to relax.

Gregor drove swiftly and well into the town, down a side street to a post office and posted the letter. Then he was back in the car again. As he leaned forward to switch on the engine he asked: 'Are you hungry?'

'Me?' She was startled. 'I don't know. Why?'

'When did you last eat?'

She had to think about that. 'I can't remember— oh yes, I had a sandwich——' she realised it was all she had eaten since the toast that morning. 'Yes, I suppose I am.' She looked at him. 'Why did you ask?'

'Because you have shadows under your eyes. It indicates tiredness or lack of food.'

'How clever! It's both. I was researching all afternoon, then typing.'

'Will you go for a meal with me?'

'Haven't you eaten either?'

'No.' Perhaps he'd been too busy to think about food. What did it matter?

'I'm not really dressed for eating out,' she looked down at her simple cotton frock. 'I'd much rather go home.'

'But will you eat then?'

'Do you care if I do or not?'

'As I am responsible for you doing a great deal of work for me—yes.'

She shrugged. 'Very well. Thank you.'

Gregor turned the car round. She realised where he was going when he left the town, and shrank back in her seat. 'Oh no, not the club. Look, I know it belongs to you, but everyone there is dressed——'

He slowed the car. 'Does that really bother you?'

'I don't know.' Her reactions were slowing down, due partly to tiredness, and certainly partly to hunger. Gregor looked at her. She was aware of the glance, and turned to him. 'I'm not being difficult. I can't think straight now.'

'Then will you leave it to me?'

'Yes, I suppose so.'

He stopped the car at the roadside, pressed a button and lifted a phone, then dialled a number. Elena listened to him speaking rapidly in Spanish, understood about one word in ten, and watched him put the phone down.

'I know this is a silly question,' she said, 'but have you just arranged a meal?'

'Yes. You understood?'

'No. I guessed, that's all. But I don't see——'

'You will.' He turned to her. 'Relax. Close your eyes if you wish. We shall eat at your house or mine, whichever you prefer.'

'Ah, I *see*. We're going to a Chinese takeaway.'

He laughed. 'There are none on the island. But you have the right idea.'

'Well, wake me when we get there. I can't wait.' She closed her eyes again, and a few minutes later he started up the car.

She should have known, she really should have guessed. He drove to his own night club, and as they purred up to the entrance two waiters came out

with a heavy box and put it carefully in the back.
Elena closed her eyes and fell asleep. When she
woke up Gregor was helping her out of the car and
taking her keys from her. 'Go and sit down in your
kitchen,' he said, 'and leave everything to me.'

'Right, I will.' She cleared his papers from the
table, but left him to move the typewriter, and she
sat and watched him unload the box. It was all
there, all perfect, on plates covered with foil, ready
to eat. Smoked salmon with wafer-thin lemon slices,
avocados filled with prawns, a cold chicken, a bowl
of salad, two watermelons, and a meringue gateau
in a cardboard box. 'My goodness!' She gazed in awe
at the spread, and her stomach protested at having
been so neglected. 'This looks superb.'

'Then we will eat.' Gregor opened a bottle of
white wine which had been carefully wrapped in
damp tissue paper and foil, and poured out two
glasses.

'Na zdorovye.'

'Cheers.' She sipped the wine slowly, savouring
its crisp dryness, and began on the smoked salmon.
It was mouth-meltingly delicious. 'Mmm!' She
looked at him across the table. 'This deserves a better setting. Candles and silverware on the dining
room table——'

'The food is more important,' he answered
gravely, 'and the company.'

He raised his glass. Elena bent her head to her
plate, confused. For some reason he was being
charming. Probably because she had done the

typing for him—and because his frustration of the morning had been forgotten. She wondered who the woman had been. His mistress—or one of several? And if Negra hadn't interrupted them, she would most probably have been added to the harem.

'Excuse me,' she said suddenly, and rose.

She went to the toilet at the end of the hall, fighting a rising sickness. She looked at her face in the mirror. She had gone pale. She splashed her face with cold water from the tap, dabbed it dry, and went back to the kitchen. Gregor stood up as she went in.

'Are you not well?'

'I'm fine,' she lied. 'Really. Please sit down.' But it was disconcerting to see the expression on his face. He was too shrewd by far. She managed to smile at him. 'This is absolutely delicious. I really must try to eat more regularly.'

'You do not eat enough. You are too slender.'

And I suppose you like your women with a bit more flesh on them, she thought. It didn't stop you this morning, did it? 'Yes, I know,' she answered. 'But when I'm writing I tend to forget about food. I live on coffee.' It was time to change the subject 'Did it take you long to write your first chapter?'

'A week, no more.' He shrugged, and helped himself to the avocado.

'That's not bad going for a beginner. Had you written anything before?'

'No. I did not really think it would be publishable. I wrote it only for a reason.'

'To get it out of your system?'

His eyes met hers across the table. There was a pause. 'Something like that,' he answered softly.

It was happening again. Tension building up—but tension of a different kind. This had nothing to do with sex. It was subtly and terribly different, yet there had been nothing in his words—or had there?

She rushed on, because any silence would be unbearable. 'But you must have a very busy life with your hotel and night club?'

'They are both run very competently by my staff.' He frowned slightly. 'But who told you about the hotel?'

'Madame Rossi, when we lunched there.' Was that only yesterday? It didn't seem possible. So much had happened. . . .

'Ah, our good mayor's wife.' He laughed. 'She is a walking computer. What she doesn't know about everyone's business isn't worth knowing.'

And she would have known my father, Elena thought. 'Has she lived on the island all her life?' she asked gently.

'Yes. I am occasionally invited to official parties of theirs.' He shrugged. 'I get out of as many as I can, of course.'

'Don't you like parties?'

'Not that kind. Standing round making small talk with boring people I have never met before and probably will never meet again is not my idea of spending a pleasant evening.'

Then what is, I wonder? Making love? But she didn't say it. 'I know what you mean.'

'Do you?'

'Do I what?'

'Like parties?'

'Sometimes, with the right people.' She cut herself a piece of chicken and helped herself to the crisp salad.

'Some more wine?' He held the bottle questioningly.

'No, thanks.'

'And what are the "right people" for you?' he enquired softly.

It was a disconcerting question. 'My friends,' she answered. 'Those I can relax with—those whose company I enjoy.'

'Of course. That is my opinion.'

'You have many friends?'

His answer surprised her. 'No.'

She raised a disbelieving eyebrow. 'You know everybody——'

'Perhaps. In my line of business I have to. This is not the same as having friends. Perhaps I am too particular, but I am more of a loner than anything else.'

'I find that hard to believe,' she said.

'Why?' Again a disconcerting question. And she had only started the conversation to avoid a tense silence.

She shook her head. 'I'm sorry—I'm getting personal.'

'No, you intrigue me. Please say what you think.'

How could she? How could she say—I've seen what happens to women when they get near you, and I too know why, because you are physically the most attractive man I've ever met, and don't you know *why*?

'I would have thought——' she was stumbling over her words, '—that you would need people round you—you have the kind of personality that —that sparks off a reaction in others.' It was said. God, what a fool he must think her!

'I don't need people,' he said slowly. 'But thank you for the compliment. And you—I think you are the same. You are very beautiful. People must like you.'

No, I'm not, I'm ugly inside because I came here seeking revenge, hating you, she wanted to cry. 'Thank you. But perhaps, like you, I'm choosy.'

'Then we are two of a kind?'

'I'm a woman—I'm different.'

'I know you are a woman, that is obvious.' He raised his glass and drank to her. 'And you have a man's brain.'

She laughed. 'That's rather patronising, don't you think? My brain's mine.'

'Forgive me, it was not intended to be so. I phrased it badly. I think you are extremely clever to write what you do.'

She shook her head. 'It comes fairly easily to me. Oh, it's work, don't get me wrong. But writing's a gift like any other. I'm just lucky I can write and get paid for it. I certainly can't sew or arrange flowers or do any of the traditional womanly occupations.' She looked at him. 'You have the gift—but I think you must already know that. Your first chapter has a power and force that comes over in every line. You're a natural.' She paused. 'Do you know what I thought when I read it?'

'No. What did you think?'

It was going to be difficult, but it had to be said: 'What you've done is better than anything I've ever written in my life.'

There was a silence that stretched and grew taut, until she thought she wouldn't be able to bear it a second longer. She saw his eyes, saw what was in them, and it was like pain. Dear God, she thought, what have I said? She stood up and went over to the sink, because she couldn't sit there a moment longer. She heard a small exclamation of sound, a movement, and then that treacherous tingling in her blood warned her that he was behind her. She felt stifled, panicky, and half turned. Did he think she had *insulted* him? What did——

He was there. He was close, much too close, and he caught her arms and held her, and she murmured: 'I'm sorry——' because she didn't know what else to say; his nearness frightened her, yet there was no danger in it. But what *was* it? He was like a man in torment. She began to tremble. Then he spoke, his voice husky. 'Why do you tremble so?'

'I don't know—I—what I said——' She shivered,

and Gregor put his arms round her and held her.

'What you said—affected me strangely. I did not mean to frighten you.'

'Why?' It was a mere whisper, a breath of sound.

'Because one day, you will know why I have written it.'

His words didn't make sense, yet they held a significance that filled her with a strange sensation of knowing.

Elena closed her eyes. She was weak again, with his nearness. She didn't want him to kiss her, yet she didn't want to stop him. And here, now, there was no Negra to interrupt. If he kissed her now....

He gave a low throaty murmur, and the next moment his lips were on hers, cool, firm, demanding. Her response was immediate and treacherous. She put her hands up to hold his face to draw it even closer, knowing that the touch of his skin delighted her more than anything she had ever known. Then softly she moved her hands round his neck and held him tighter still. Their bodies were as one, on fire, she a-tingle with the warmth of him, the sheer hard virile muscularity and strength. She was safe now, safer than she had ever been before in the world, and this was the only place she ever wanted to be. His lips moved to touch her cheeks, her mouth, her chin in a butterfly caress, while his hands stroked her body with a sensuality and expertise that took the last remnants of her sanity away.

He groaned something, and his lips found hers

again, and she tasted the salt sweetness of his mouth, and was lost. Then suddenly he moved, stood back, only inches, but a world away.

'No,' he said huskily. He released her and turned away, and Elena stood there, ready to fall, and felt as if part of her had been torn away from her. She reached out to touch his arm, and he turned to her. 'No,' he said again. 'Let me go.'

Her breath was tortured, she went dizzy. 'Let you go?' she mumbled, still dazed——Gregor turned away, shoulders bowed as if in pain, and she felt a surge of anger, of rejection——

'Get out,' she breathed. 'Get *out* of here!'

He walked out, and she heard the door close behind him. She put her hands to her head and cried.

CHAPTER SIX

WHEN morning came Elena was exhausted. She had slept little, and when she had the dreams had been so disturbing that she had woken from them drenched in perspiration. She felt ill, and wretched. After a shower she felt a little better, took two aspirins, and had a cup of coffee. It was not yet seven o'clock, and the day seemed to stretch ahead in a yawning blank. Elena looked in dismay at the clock on the wall. She knew she must shake herself out of this mood of depression and get some writing done. It was Wednesday, and either on Friday evening or early Saturday, Jerry would be returning. It seemed her one lifeline. And if she had something to show for her days there, he would feel pleased. She had managed to block Gregor from out of her mind, but here in the kitchen were reminders of him—the remains of the food, the plates from the night club, the half-empty bottle of wine—and his manuscript.

She looked at it. She didn't want to touch anything that belonged to him. She had made a complete fool of herself—and he had rejected her. Then, in a blinding flash of realisation, she knew why. 'My God,' she said softly, 'that's it!' He had exacted a sweet subtle revenge for what had happened on the beach. And how gently he had led up to it! The meal, the pleasant conversation, then the kiss. She had thought her words had had an effect on him, but now, in the clear light of day, she realised that he had been waiting his chance. If it hadn't been then, it would have been at some other moment, equally opportune. How clever, she thought. How very clever of him. The look of pain in his eyes, calculated to bewilder her, the growing silence, until she was confused, and then—pow! One trembling girl, ready and ripe for seduction. He'd probably laughed all the way to bed.

At least we're quits, she thought. She was resilient, already beginning to bounce back. Oh yes, you're clever, she thought. But not as clever as me, because now I know.

She would start the book today, and the character of Count Igor Vassily was going to be so real it would be frightening. Once that was decided, the day assumed a brighter aspect. Jerry was going to get a surprise at the weekend. She stood up and cleared all the plates into the box that Gregor had bought, took his manuscript and the carbon copy and pushed them in an empty drawer in the kitchen, then went upstairs, lighter of heart.

She spread her books out on the desk, selected her favourite pen, and opened the exercise book. 'Chapter one' she wrote with a flourish, then, remembering, she wrote above that: 'The Romanov Way.' She underlined it carefully, then began to write. She didn't need to make notes about the

Count. She had everything she needed all ready in her mind to spill out on paper. So vivid were the images that her mind raced on faster than her pen could put the words down. That had never happened before, in any book.

She heard the front door open, and the housekeeper's voice. 'Mees Kingdon?'

'I'm here, *señora*, upstairs. Just a moment, I'll come down.' She needed a break. Her hand ached from writing, and she was thirsty. She ran down and the little woman smiled at her and thrust letters at her.

'The post—for you,' she said.

'Oh, thank you.' Elena smiled at her. She hadn't given the post a thought, although generally in England there was mail every day, fan letters, cards from friends, invitations to speak at writers' groups. . . .

'I'm making a coffee for myself. Would you like one?'

'Ah, yes, please. Then I work. Is there anything you wish me to do today?'

'Well, yes. I have a friend staying at the weekend. Would you see that there is a bedroom cleaned and ready?'

'Certainly.' Button-black eyes and a big smile made Elena respond. Señora Bonita was a cheerful little soul; Jerry had told Elena that she had six grown-up children. She didn't look old enough to even be married. Perhaps it's the air, thought Elena. . . .

'There is a box in the corner belonging to Mr Vlados,' Elena told her as she lifted the kettle. 'Perhaps you could return it later when you've finished work. If he's not in, just leave it on the step. He'll find it.'

'Sure, sure, okay.'

'And there's a meringue cake in the fridge. Would you like to take that home with you?'

'Oh, please!'

That's that, she thought. And if he wants his manuscript back, he can come and ask for it. They drank coffee and the little Mexican woman practised her English on Elena by telling her all about her family. One of her sons worked in Gregor's hotel. Elena sat up mentally at that and said:

'How nice. He lives next door, you know.'

'Si, I do know. He is a very nice man, a good boss, my Tonio says.'

'Oh, I'm sure he is,' said Elena sweetly. 'Has your son worked there long?'

'Since he left school, four years now. He works in the kitchens. Meester Vlados is very good cook himself, and very particular. Everything is best quality. A lot of tourists stay at the hotel.'

He must be making a fortune, Elena thought. 'He's not married, is he? Mr Vlados, I mean,' she asked vaguely, as she sifted through the letters.

'Not yet, but——' Señora Bonita stopped and began to wave away an irritating fly, and Elena waited with bated breath. What *was* she going to say?

'But?' she prompted, very gently.

'But we wonder sometimes—there is the American lady, and the other one.'

'The other one?' echoed Elena faintly.

'*Si*. The American lady comes here regularly on business. She is a—what is the word—beauty consu——' she faltered.

'Consultant?'

'*Si*, that is it!' Señora Bonita smiled her relief. 'At one of the big stores in San Cristóbal, and she travels round North America as well, so she only comes down every few months, and the other one does not like that.'

'No, she wouldn't. Er—who is the other one?'

The housekeeper rolled her dark eyes expressively. 'Ah, Juanita Perez. She is Mexican—very beautiful.'

'She lives here, on the island?'

'*Si*. But she is away visiting her family in Mexico just at present.' Which meant that the woman in Gregor's house the previous night was yet another one. The mind boggled. Perhaps her humiliation had been exaggerated; he probably tried it on with all and sundry at the slightest opportunity. But never again, not with me you won't, she thought. She began, strangely enough, to feel better about everything.

'And you think he might marry one of them?'

'I think they both would like. They do not speak to each other.'

That was hardly surprising. 'What is the American lady's name?' Elena asked. She intended paying a visit to the store as soon as possible—very casually, of course. After all, she needed make-up....

'Loren Slinger. She is very blonde, and Juanita is very dark.'

Nothing like a bit of variety, thought Elena. Perhaps last night's was a redhead.

She finished her coffee and stood up. 'I'll get back to my work. I'm upstairs if you need me.'

She opened the letters. Two were invitations to parties, one at the Rossis', the other at some people called Ellerson. That was a handwritten invitation on expensive notepaper apologising for the short notice, but they had only just heard Miss Kingdon was on the island and there were so many people dying to meet her. The party was for the following evening, the Rossis' on Sunday. There was an airmail letter from a friend in London, Sheila, another writer, and a bill for some magazines addressed to her uncle. Elena put them on one side to deal with later, and started writing again.

The Count was emerging as a strong character, taking shape nicely. She was very surprised to find, suddenly, that it was growing dark, and looked at her watch to see it was nearly six. Stiff from sitting so long, she went downstairs to find a note on the table from Señora Bonita to say that all the work was done, she was returning the box to Señor Vlados, and she did not wish to disturb Miss Kingdon, so had left quietly.

'Mmm, good for you,' said Elena. Señora Bonita was clearly a tactful soul who appreciated that writers most definitely did not need interruptions. She decided to eat something while she was down, and telephone Madame Rossi before the Ellersons.

She was put through by a secretary, and Madame Rossi came on the line. 'Miss Kingdon, how nice of you to call. I hope you will be able to come on Sunday? We will send a car for you, of course.'

'I'd like that. My publisher may be here—you met him at lunch. May I bring him as well?'

'How delightful, but of course.'

'Madame Rossi,' Elena added, 'I've been invited to a party by some people called Ellerson. Do you know them?'

An amused little laugh came down the line. 'The Americans, ah yes—I wondered how long it would be. They are very—what is the expression—high society, very important.'

'Ah, do you think I'll enjoy it?'

'I'm *sure* you will, my dear. They will make a big fuss of you—and they have a very handsome son, a lovely boy.'

'Oh, thanks for telling me. I'll see you on Sunday. I'm looking forward to it.'

'As we are to having you. Goodbye for now.'

'Goodbye, Madame.' Elena put the telephone down, grinned, and picked it up again to dial Mrs Ellerson. Then she went upstairs to write for a while longer. Life on the island was getting slightly more organized. She was writing well. That was the most important thing—and she was going to meet new people, which could only be good for her, under the circumstances. And the less she saw of her neighbour the better.

Yet it was strange, but as she went to bed later that night, utterly exhausted from all the writing she had done, she felt as if something had been missing from the day. She had not seen Gregor at all since the previous night. Not once. Most odd. She didn't miss him, and since hearing about various of his women, she had been sharply cured of her brief infatuation. And yet in a way the day had been empty, like a meal without salt.

She punched her pillow and lay down on her side to watch the moon over the trees. Tomorrow was planned. She would get up early and write for a while, then she would drive into San Cristobál and buy some clothes and food for the weekend. Thus planning, she drifted off into a deep sleep.

Señora Bonita assured Elena that the best shop for dresses was the one called Adam's. She didn't tell her it belonged to Gregor; Elena only found that out when she was trying on dresses. She emerged from the changing room to see if the assistant could have the dress she had chosen taken in a fraction, and saw him standing talking to the woman. The shock was almost physical, and she caught her breath. He turned slowly, as if he had been waiting for her, and said: 'Good afternoon, Elena.'

'Good afternoon.' She nodded to him, then spoke

to the assistant, whose English was good. 'Is it possible to have the dress altered today, please? It needs taking in slightly just here.' She touched the silky black jersey where it covered her hips. It was a slim-fitting, figure-shaping dress, full-length, with narrow diamanté shoulder straps, and she knew it was the one she wanted the moment she tried it on, but her hips were too slender.

'Ah, *señorita!*' the woman shook her head doubtfully, 'today? I think——' Gregor said something to her in Spanish and her face immediately changed. 'But yes, of course. One moment, please, I will fetch the fitter.' And she darted off.

'Don't tell me this place belongs to you as well,' said Elena dryly.

'Yes, it does. Don't worry, I have told her they are to do it for you. In fact, if you have any further shopping to do, you can call back in an hour for it. It will be ready, I guarantee that.'

'That's very kind of you.'

'It is my pleasure.' But his expression belied his words.

'I shall wait. I've done my shopping.' It was nearly five, and she looked at her watch. 'I'm going to a party.' She hoped it might annoy him.

'I know.'

She looked sharply at him. 'You *know*? But I only got the invitation yesterday.'

'News travels fast. I know most things.'

'I'm sure you do,' she smiled. The assistant returned with a smaller, overall-clad woman carrying tape measure and pincushion, and Gregor said something again to her, and she nodded.

'Si, señor. Si.' He walked away.

The measuring took only a few minutes, and Elena went to get her dress off and change. When she came out to pay the assistant said:

'Will you come this way, please?'

'Oh—where to? To pay?'

'Yes. This way, señorita.' She took her through a door marked 'No Entrada,' and Elena followed her up some stairs to where she knocked at a plain green door and waited. The door was opened by Gregor, who said: 'Come in, Elena,' and to the woman, 'Muchas gracias, Maria.'

She walked into a large comfortable office with a desk, several chairs, a huge palm in the corner and a wide window giving a view of the main street, including the Hotel Plaza.

'Please sit down,' he said. He wore more sober clothes today, dark trousers and white shirt, open-necked, and a thin dark jacket. He looked very tanned, probably in contrast with the whiteness of his shirt.

'I'm not stopping. I have more shopping to do,' said Elena, and remained standing. He walked away from her towards the window, then turned to face her.

'But you said you had finished it.'

'I changed my mind.' She regarded him coolly.

'And how long will you be?'

'The dress will take an hour, you said. I'll come

back at six.'

'Are you in your car?'

'Yes. It's parked round the corner. Don't tell me you own the car park as well?'

He smiled. 'No. But I would like to ask you a favour.'

'What is it?'

'Will you give me a lift home? My Rolls has gone to be serviced and it won't be ready until tomorrow.'

She wanted to say no. She could, quite easily. 'All right.'

'Thank you.'

'Don't mention it. I'll be back in an hour.'

'The dress will be waiting for you.'

'I'm sure it will. You will be too, I take it?'

'Yes.'

'The woman wouldn't let me pay. I thought she was bringing me up here to do so.' Elena opened her bag. 'How much is the dress in English money?'

'I shall have to work it out. I'll let you know when you return.'

'Very well.' She went towards the door and he stepped past her and opened it. 'Goodbye.'

'Goodbye.'

She sailed out, found the stairs and went down the one flight into the store again. She spent the next hour trying out perfumes and make-up. She wondered if this was where the American Loren Slinger worked. It was quite possible. How convenient for them both if so. She thought she had handled the little scene in his office with dignity and complete coolness. She hoped so, anyway.

She made sure she was back in the gown department before six, because she had the faint suspicion that Gregor had intended letting her have the dress for nothing, or at least with a heavy discount, and she had no intention of letting him. She would not be under any obligation to him.

She found her assistant, who produced the dress. Elena tried it on, with the needlewoman clucking anxiously round her, and it was perfect. It fitted like a dream. 'Thank you, that's marvellous,' she said. 'Please let me have the bill. I'll just go and take it off.' It was ten to six. She hurriedly dressed and went out, they wrapped the dress up and put it in a box, and she said: 'Now, please, how much, with the alterations?'

'There is no charge, *señorita*.'

'Oh—for the alterations? That's very kind. But how much for the dress?'

'No, that is for the dress. No charge. Señor Vlados's instructions——'

'But I'm paying—' Elena stopped. The assistant was looking uncomfortable, and while she wasn't exactly wringing her hands she might do so at any minute, if pushed.

'I see. Where is Señor Vlados?'

'I have phoned through. He is on his way.'

'Thank you, I'll wait.' She watched the door, and watched—then the fatal tingle warned her, and she turned, and he was behind her. She took a deep breath. 'Oh! I want a word——'

'Yes,' he took her arm, 'of course you do. This way.' He guided her through the department, watched discreetly by all the staff and not a few customers, and Elena wondered what would happen if she started arguing with him there. She had absolutely no intention of doing so. But when they were in her car——

She opened the driver's door and got in, flinging her dress on the back seat. Then she turned to face him. 'I don't know what your game is,' she said, 'but you don't buy me with a dress. I'm going to pay for it——'

'It is a small return for the work you did.'

'The typing? Don't be ridiculous!' she snapped. 'Good grief, I'd need to type ten books for you before I paid for that. I'm independent, you know. I don't need your charity or your favours.' Her eyes sparkled her anger, and her cheeks were pink. 'God knows what those assistants thought of me. That I was another of your mistresses, I suppose—well, I'm not, and I'm not going to be.'

'Have you finished?' he said quietly. He wasn't angry, he was smouldering.

'Nearly. You can't buy people, you know. You can't buy *me*.'

She started the engine and eased her way out from the row of cars in the parking lot. She was angry, but she'd had her say. She had told him. She drove out into the road and turned into the main street, and along. Gregor sat beside her cold and silent, and gradually her mood changed. Faintly horrified, she remembered what she had said, and the force of her words. And what had he answered: 'It is a small return for the work you did.' Perhaps that was all he meant, no more. Her own strong feelings of love, hate, all mingled, had provided the rest. She drove on, now anguished, and when they reached her front door, she got out and said: 'You'd better come in for your manuscript. I'd hate it to get lost.'

He said not a word, watched her fumble for her key, and followed her in. Elena went straight into the kitchen and opened the drawer where she had flung the papers and took them out. Then she swallowed, and said:

'Look, I might have been a bit hasty——'

'You were. But don't fear, you will get the bill tomorrow—I shall see to it personally.' His eyes were glacial, contemptuous.

'I'm sorry,' she said.

'I do not allow anyone to speak to me as you did,' he went on, as if she hadn't spoken. 'It was not a question of "buying" you, as you put it. The dress is nothing to me—part of stock—it was a gesture of gratitude, that was all. Yet you immediately assumed the worst. And what precisely did you mean about my mistresses?'

'If you don't know, I don't intend to tell you,' she answered. 'I've only heard about two, so perhaps I'm not qualified to speak on the subject.'

'Two? Who are they?'

She turned away. 'Please go. I'm getting ready for a party.'

'I know you are. But I'm not going to go until you've finished what you started.'

'What I started? Huh, that's rich! I've seen you in action—God, you're clever! You can twist things round, can't you——' He caught her wrist and held it tightly.

'Tell me what you mean,' he said oh, so quietly, and she was frightened.

'Let me go,' she breathed.

'When you have answered me.'

'No, I won't! Don't think you can use force——'

'I would like to beat you——' His voice shook with anger.

'I'll bet you would too. Is that how you get your kicks? Ouch—you're hurting!'

'Not as much as I would like to.'

Elena swung her free arm round and fetched him a resounding slap on his face, then arched her body to try and free herself. Gregor caught and swung her round, imprisoning her in his arms. His voice was husky and excited. 'Listen to me, listen well. You are capable of making me more angry than anyone else ever has, or ever will. I cannot beat you—much as you need it—but I will find some other way to punish you, never fear.'

'If you think—you'll f-frighten me talking like that, you're——' her voice faltered, then failed. She hated herself for it, but the very struggle in itself was an excitement that coursed through her blood.

She had never been so aware of a man as she was of him. It was something quite beyond her power of control. And he knew it as well as she did. She wondered, fleetingly, if it was because she had the same effect on him—and found out a moment later when he turned her round, crushed her to him, and groaning, said:

'Oh God, you could drive me wild!'

She was locked against him, against his heart, feeling the strong steady beat, quickening, pulsing against her until it filled her very being with its rhythm.

Then he pushed her away abruptly, looked at her, his eyes dark and hard, and said softly: 'Be thankful you are a woman.'

She laughed, saw his face change, but she couldn't stop herself. She had a heady sense of power, for an instant, then it was gone as he reached for her and kissed her with a savage intensity that took the breath from her body. He bruised her lips with his, with the sheer force of them, and when he had done her mouth was throbbing and sore. She put her hand to her burning face. The skin tingled with the pressure from his beard shadow, and was raw. 'You hurt me,' she whispered.

'Yes, but not as much as I would have liked.' He turned and walked steadily away. 'Be ready at nine.'

'Nine? What for? *I'm* going to——'

'To the Ellersons'. They said you would have a car sent. It's mine.' Elena gaped at him, speechless. 'I'm going too,' he explained. 'Didn't they tell you?'

'You don't like parties——'

'I go to some. I'm going to this.'

'What in? Mine?'

'No, mine. I have three cars. Be ready.'

'I don't want to go with you——' she began.

'You have no choice.'

She went after him, reached him at the door. 'Do you think I'd enjoy it, with you?' she demanded. 'After—after *that*?'

Gregor looked down at her. 'You'll enjoy it.'

'And after? I suppose *you'll* be bringing me back?'

'I wouldn't let you walk.'

'It might be preferable. I've been in a car with you at night, remember?'

'I shan't touch you,' he assured her.

'Hah! How do I know?'

'You don't.' He put his hand up and ran it down her cheek. 'You'll just have to hope——'

'Hope for what? For you to behave yourself? I don't think you're capable.'

'When you behave yourself, so will I. When you provoke me——'

'I don't!' She sparked fire at him.

'You are provocative just standing there. You are maddening, unpredictable——'

'I could say the same about you!'

'Then we understand each other, don't we?'

'No! I'll never understand you—I don't want to. Just go, now——'

'I intend to,' he drawled. 'Be ready.'

'I'll be ready, but I've not decided if I'll let you take me yet. I might phone them——'

'And what will you say? "I don't like my neighbour—I don't want him to bring me?" They know me; they don't know you. Think about it. Imagine the speculation.' She could.

'It'll give them something to think about.'

'Indeed it will.' He smiled softly. 'I wonder what?'

'You're despicable!' she breathed.

'I think not.' He looked at his watch. 'Don't be late. It should be an interesting party.'

'Why?' she whispered. 'Why——'

Gregor knew what the question meant. He didn't need to ask her. 'Because—because you—and I—will learn, one day, to understand one another; and then you will know that you hated me without reason or sense.' He walked out and left her standing there bereft of speech.

Elena turned and walked slowly back to the kitchen, eyes wide, dazed. Gregor had said things before that dismayed her. But what he had said just now passed that. It entered into realms about which she dared hardly think. For it was almost as though he knew everything about her. He was frightening—and he was fascinating.

CHAPTER SEVEN

ELENA washed her hair and had a cool shower, then went down clad in a towel robe to eat a sandwich and drink a glass of milk while her hair dried. She had her beauty routine planned. She was going to look stunning, and she was going to have an absolutely wonderful time at the party, and she would teach Gregor Vlados a lesson. She would go with him because she had no choice, but she would spend no time at all with him during the evening, and if she didn't feel like coming home with him, she wouldn't.

She had bought make-up and perfume. She generally wore little, but tonight there was going to be quite a difference in her appearance. She knew all the tricks with eye-shadows and blushers. She had a friend who was a photographic model, and had watched her get ready for a modelling session many a time, and marvelled at the skill and expertise that went into making the 'natural' look. So this evening, with nearly an hour to spare, she was going to use all her knowledge. She smiled a little smile to herself, and went upstairs to spread the various items out on the dressing table. Then she sat down with a towel round her shoulders, a thin chiffon scarf keeping her hair from her face, looked at herself in the mirror, and began.

I certainly wouldn't like to do this every day, she thought, half an hour later. She was nearly finished, was applying the third and final coat of sooty black mascara to her already thick eyelashes. She sat back and looked at herself critically. 'Mmm, that's nearly it,' she said, and smoothed the final touch, the shiny white pearl eye-shadow just beneath her eyebrows. Her eyes looked larger and more luminous than ever before. Her face was cool, tanned loveliness, the blusher faintly accentuating her cheekbones. Her mouth was pink shimmering perfection —helped, oddly enough, by the bruising kiss from Gregor, which had softened her lips, made them tender. 'Golly, you're *gorgeous*!' she breathed, and grinned impishly at her reflection.

Her timing was perfect. As she walked down the stairs, trailing the cobwebby golden stole that went like a dream with the dress, there was a tap on the door. She paused, and called: 'Come in,' then waited. Gregor walked in, looked up, saw her—and stopped. He didn't need to say anything. She saw the effect she had on him by the expression in his eyes, and that was enough, more than enough. She went down the last few steps and faced him, and smiled. 'Good evening,' she said. 'You're early.'

'Yes. What have you done?'

'Done?' She looked behind her, as if he might possibly be speaking to someone else, then back. 'What *do* you mean?'

'You look—different. Very different.'

'Ah! You like it? I decided I'd try a bit of the make-up I bought at your store. Just a dab of eye-shadow, you know,' she smiled innocently. 'Doesn't it suit me?'

'Yes. If you're ready, we'll go.'

Elena looked properly at him. He too was differ-ent, very different—devastating in an evening suit. Broad-shouldered, a magnificent animal. My God, she thought, he'll bowl 'em over like ninepins—and a pang of jealousy pierced her suddenly. She turned away and walked towards the kitchen, leav-ing a trail of 'Chamade' in the air. She had bought that today as well. It had always done things for her, and she had put the perfume spray in her evening bag so that she could apply more before they arrived.

She switched on the alarm, called out: 'I'm going to have a glass of milk before I go.' Gregor fol-lowed her in.

'Milk?'

'Yes. Do you want a glass? It helps keep you sober.'

'I don't need milk to do that.' He watched her pour the glass of ice-cold milk from the refrigera-tor. 'I drink very little.'

'So you do! I forgot. How nice to have such iron self-control—or can't you take it?'

A smile touched the corner of his wide mouth. 'I don't need it.'

'Nor do I, but if you can't drink at a party, when can you?'

'True, but then I'm driving. You'd feel safer with a sober driver, surely?'

She gave a little laugh. 'I haven't decided if you're bringing me home yet. It all depends——'

Gregor raised one eyebrow and his mouth quirked. 'On what?'

She shrugged. 'On whether I see anyone I'd prefer——'

'*I* drive you home.'

'Do you indeed? We're not even there yet.'

'Then we might as well get it clear before we are,' he said. 'The arrangement is made. It stands.'

'We'll see about it.' Elena drank the milk carefully so as not to mar her lipstick. 'Let's go.'

She floated past him, the golden stole swirling casually, and turned back to smile at him. 'We'll try and be nice to one another on our way there. That will make a change.'

He didn't answer. He followed her out and slammed the door shut. Laughing softly, Elena opened the door of the Maserati and got in.

Gregor drove carefully down the long drive, then opened up speed on the road. He was a fast driver, skilful and careful. She sat back and relaxed, wondering what the evening would hold, and the journey was accomplished in silence.

The line of cars as they approached the large house would have told of a party in progress even without the bright lights and music streaming out from open windows and doors. Gregor parked behind a Jaguar and got out to open Elena's door.

They walked up a gravelly drive, he striding out, she having to run to keep up with him, and went into a large crowded hall. Heads turned, voices greeted him, Elena blinked at the brightness of it all, and then a tall, distinguished woman detached herself from a knot of people and came forward to greet them, kissing Gregor warmly, turning to Elena. 'My dear Miss Kingdon, how kind of you to come to our little gathering.' She took her hand and shook it. 'May I say that you look absolutely radiant? I'm Lois Ellerson.'

She wore a deceptively simple oyster satin dress, high-necked, long-sleeved, and a diamond pendant was her only jewellery. She needed no more. Blue-eyed, flawless complexion, she was about fifty and looked thirty. But her smile was warm and genuine.

'I'm glad to meet you,' answered Elena.

'Come on, my dear, I'll introduce you round. So many people *dying* to meet the celebrity. Gregor darling, Larry wants a word with you, though God knows where he is. You'll find him?'

'I'll find him,' Gregor assured her gravely, and as they walked away from him, he was pounced on by two attractive women who kissed him, laughing delightedly.

'He's so popular,' whispered Lois Ellerson. 'My *God*, it was such a surprise when he said he'd like to come! I must make sure he has a good evening, it's such a cachet to have him at one's parties. Thanks to you! Though looking at you, I know why,' and she laughed huskily. Then, before Elena could think about the precise significance of what her hostess had just unwittingly told her, she was being introduced to everybody. She knew she wouldn't remember any names, but she was used to that. The secret was to smile charmingly, to talk for a while, and to keep moving. A white-gloved waitress handed her a glass of champagne, and Elena greeted the men and women, all immaculate, all beautiful people, 'jet-setters,' all charming, and all talking at once. Lois Ellerson left her with a couple while she darted off to greet some new-comers, promising to return, and Elena talked to them as though she had wanted to meet them for a long time. Jack and Ellen Freeman, Americans, Ellen quite overcome at meeting a real live author, and she had also read Elena's books and *loved* them.

'My goodness, when I tell them back in Boysie that I met you, they'll be *green*,' she shrilled. 'Say, your first book, that was a wow! Tell me, honey, where do you get your *ideas*?'

It was a question Elena was used to. She could guarantee to hear it at least once at every party. She smiled modestly and began to explain that it was a question of sitting down and plotting and plan-ning, and then 'something takes over, you know.' By this time several more had joined the little group, until she thought, amused, I'm giving a talk on writing here!

More questions were fired at her, then a tall handsome man moved nearer, and listened; she knew who it was because the likeness to his mother was unmistakable. Hmm, she thought, even as she mouthed the words they wanted to hear, not bad, not bad at all. Madame Rossi had been right: he was very attractive.

He took advantage of a lull in the talk and questions, to hand her a drink and say: 'Hi, I'm Chuck.'

'Hello.' He looked round, and the crowd melted away, smiling, charming as ever, murmuring, 'we must talk again,' and they were alone, in a little oasis of quiet.

'Do you always get rid of people so quickly?' Elena murmured, laughing.

'It's a gift.' He grinned at her. 'You don't really want to be stuck in a group all evening telling them about your books, do you?'

'It might help to sell a few,' she retorted, mock-indignant. 'A girl has to earn a living, you know.'

'I'll buy a few thousand, then you can talk to me.'

'Oh, what about?'

'About—are you going to dance with me?'

'Is there dancing?'

'Sure is. Can't you hear the music? Come on,' he took her arm, removed her empty glass and deposited it on a passing tray. 'I'll show you where.'

They were already dancing in a large room at the back of the white mansion. An open wall led out to a stone-flagged terrace, lit with dozens of fairy lights strung from the trees, and some couples were even dancing on the lawn. It was a fairytale picture. The music came from a four-man band seated on a platform at the end, and the samba beat was catchy and compelling.

Chuck Ellerson swung her into his arms. 'Let's go,' he said, and whirled her away, laughing, into the crowd. He was amusing, and good company. But he wasn't Gregor. To her own faint horror, Elena found herself searching for him even as she did a waltz a few minutes later, and Chuck was holding her close.

He stayed by her side all evening, and there were at least a hundred people at the party, and she met virtually everyone, was treated like royalty, and was having an absolutely magnificent evening. The drink flowed freely, the buffet supper was superb, she was constantly surrounded by people, and she glimpsed Gregor only from a distance where he was always accompanied by several of his own admirers—all female, she thought sourly. She sipped a glass of champagne, listening only with one ear to Chuck discussing something with a fellow American, and thought, I intended to teach him a lesson, only he's not let me. Yet she was aware of him constantly. He was *there*. It was odd, she couldn't explain it, but she was nerve-tinglingly aware that he was never too far away. She saw him dancing once, laughing, with a strikingly dark-haired beauty in white, and she looked away before he could see her glance.

At one the party was still going strong, but Elena was wilting. She sat in a comparatively quiet corner and took off her shoes for a minute while Chuck went to find her another drink. A man came out of the crowd and she focussed her eyes to see Gregor watching her.

'Why, hello!' she said. 'Fancy seeing *you* here.'

'You are tired?'

'Whatever makes you think that? You're not, I take it?'

He smiled faintly. 'No. Are you ready to leave?'

'Soon. But don't worry, I won't draw *you* away from the party. Chuck will take me.'

A twitch, no more, at the corner of his wide mouth. 'Has he said?'

'Yes.' She smiled at him very sweetly. 'I told you, didn't——' she stopped as Chuck returned bearing two glasses, and grinned at Gregor.

'Hi,' he said. 'Want one of these?'

Gregor shook his head. 'No, thanks. It was very kind of you to offer to run Elena home, Chuck, but I think we'll leave now. I'll just go and have a word with your mother before we leave.' He smiled in a most charming way at the young American and walked away.

Chuck looked at her in comic dismay, and handed her the glass. 'You said——' he began.

'I know.' She was furious and disturbed. 'I thought he was staying on, and I'm a little tired——'

'You heard the man. He's taking you now.' He gave a wry grin. 'He's the boss.'

She looked at him. That was it: one word from Gregor—and the subject was closed. 'Tell him *you're* taking me,' she said huskily.

'You're kidding. Didn't you see his face?'

'No. Did you?' she answered shortly.

'Yep. He brought you, he takes you home—his eyes said it for him.' He gave a low whistle. 'Sorry, honey, I'll call you tomorrow. Can I?'

'I'll be writing.' She drank the champagne in one swallow, and the bubbles went up her nose, making her eyes water. *'Ooh!'* She had gone right off Chuck. Was he a man or a mouse? A mouse, undoubtedly. She squinted up at him, then Gregor came back, weaving a way skilfully through the crowds drinking and talking.

'We'll leave now,' he said. 'Lois is by the door waiting to see us off.' He put a hand on Chuck's shoulder. 'Thanks for looking after Elena,' he said. 'You've done a great job. Can we have lunch tomorrow? Plaza—say one o'clock?'

Chuck's face lit up. 'Sure. Fine.' They shook hands, and Gregor took Elena's arm in a solicitous way and guided her through the guests. She nodded and smiled her goodnights, and they parted respectfully for her and Gregor, then they were in the hall.

'Mrs Ellerson, I've had a *lovely* evening. Thank you *so* much!' Elena laid it on thick, because she was more than somewhat tipsy and she was furious with Gregor and she was going to give him *hell* in the car, and she didn't care.

'My dear, you will come again? I'll be in touch. It's been absolutely *delightful*, having you here.' She kissed Elena warmly on the cheek, then kissed

Gregor, and Elena thought, oh, that's lovely, everyone loves everyone else—then they were outside, she weaving slightly as they walked down the gravel drive, and Gregor took her arm, laughing silently.

She shook his arm free as they neared the car, and hissed: 'You despicable *beast*! I hate you!'

'Yes, I know.' He helped her in, tucking her skirt well inside, slammed her door, then went to his own. Inside he looked at her. 'You are drunk,' he said.

'Go to *hell*!' She lashed out and caught him a stinging blow, but he caught her hands and kissed her. Then he released her and started the car. He was still laughing.

She sat in furious, stony silence all the way, and he went up the drive and stopped the car. 'Get your keys,' he said gently, 'and I'll carry you in to bed. You're scarcely fit to walk——'

'Get lost!' She slammed out of the car and ran up the steps, fumbling in her bag, followed by Gregor. Then she opened the bag wide and shook it and stood looking at it in dazed dismay.

'Oh God!' she moaned.

'Don't tell me, let me guess. You've forgotten your keys—right?'

'I——' she remembered where they were. On her dressing table next to the perfume, ready to pick up. Only she had picked up the perfume, put some on, and hadn't picked up the keys.

Gregor took the bag from her. 'May I?' He delved in. 'No.'

'Oh!' In a small voice, she said: 'What shall I do?'

'Sleep on the step?' he suggested. 'What a good job Chuck didn't bring you. You'd have looked a bit foolish rolling back to the party after making such a splendid exit.'

She sat down on the step, her legs like jelly. 'Goodnight,' she said with great dignity. He sat beside her.

'You don't have much choice,' he said gently. 'You will have to sleep at my house.'

She looked at him. 'You must be *joking*!'

'You will be quite safe. I have no taste for seducing drunken women.'

'I'm *not* drunk!'

'You are. How many did you have?'

'I can't remember.'

'I can,' he drawled. 'At least ten glasses.'

'How do *you* know? I never saw you——'

'But I saw *you*. I made very sure I saw you.'

'Huh!' a disbelieving snort. 'Why? *You* were too busy——'

'Because I had taken you. You were my responsibility. That is why I brought you home as well.'

'Oh yes,' she said slowly. 'You did *that* very neatly.'

'True—I intended to. He'd had too much to drink.'

'Is that why you asked him to lunch?'

'No. We have business to talk about. He's very bright, I can use him.'

'Like you use everybody?' she said bitterly.

'I am not prepared to sit here all night arguing with you. Shall we go?'

'No. I'm staying here.'

Gregor pulled her to her feet before she could even gasp. 'Do I carry you, or do you come quietly? I too am tired.'

Elena shook herself free. 'I suppose I don't have much choice.'

'No, you don't. Get in the car.'

Sullenly she obeyed, sat back and closed her eyes. When she awoke Gregor was carrying her upstairs in his house, her old house, and into her own childhood bedroom. He put her down on the bed. 'The bathroom is next door,' he said. 'Do you want anything before I go?'

'I've nothing to wear,' she said in a little voice.

'It's warm. You'll live. Goodnight.' He went out and closed the door, and she heard his footsteps going down the stairs.

She put out her tongue at the door, kicked off her shoes, and went out to the bathroom.

She laid her dress out on a chair, kept on her bra and pants, and climbed in between cool cotton sheets. Within a minute she was fast asleep.

She was awoken by a tap on the door and sat up, then remembering, pulled up the sheet.

'Come in.'

Gregor came in, fully dressed, carrying a cup and

saucer. 'Good morning,' he said. 'Did you sleep well?'

'Yes, thanks.'

'I've brought you a cup of coffee. I've been over to see your housekeeper and I have your keys here.' He took them out of his pocket and set them down, beside the coffee on the bedside cupboard. 'You can get up when you like. I have to go into town now.'

Elena looked up at him, puzzled. This was a perfectly cool stranger. No tension, no undercurrents, nothing. He stood waiting, ready for off, it seemed.

'Thank you for the coffee, and for putting me up for the night,' she said.

'A pleasure. Do you need anything before I go?'

'No, I don't think so.'

He turned, began to walk out, then: 'Oh, I nearly forgot. Jerry phoned.'

'Yes?'

He smiled. 'He had tried to call you, but got no reply. So he rang me—I had given him my number the other night.' A pause, and she knew what was coming. 'He—er—wondered where you were. So I told him.'

'You——' she had to swallow, 'told him I was here?'

'Yes. Did I not do right?'

'Hell!' She looked at him, and it was all in her eyes. 'What do *you* think?'

'He had merely called to say he will arrive about eight tonight. I explained about your lost key——'

'I'll bet you did!' In her agitation she swung the covers back, then remembered her state of undress and covered herself again.

Gregor sat down on the bed, eyes gently puzzled. 'But should I have told a lie, perhaps? Said you were out——'

'You could have forced yourself, couldn't you?'

'But he is staying with you over the weekend—is that not the same thing? After all, you are not lovers, are you?'

'That's none of your business,' she snapped.

'Then it will be quite as respectable, as your visit here is. Have I touched you? Have I offend——'

'Oh, go to hell! You know damn well what you've done, and you're loving every minute of it,' she retorted.

Gregor began to laugh, softly at first, then richly, and Elena, furious, almost beside herself with white-hot temper, tried to push him off the bed.

'Stop laughing!' she panted, 'and get away——'

'You are funny!'

'I'm *not*!' she gasped. He wasn't moving. He put his head in his hands as if he couldn't control his laughter. She swung a pillow at him, hoping vainly to dislodge him, but he caught it, pulled it, and her, towards him with a swift powerful jerk that left her sprawling half out of the bed, caught her and held her helpless, and then, no longer laughing, suddenly sober, said:

'Now struggle, you little wildcat!'

'Mmm——' She gritted her teeth and writhed

like the wildcat he had called her, wriggling, struggling mainly to free herself from a grip of steel. 'Let me *go*!'

'I have never met anyone so violent as you——' He was silenced as she bit his arm, the nearest available thing, and he swore softly. The next second she was flung back on to the bad, and Gregor was on top of her, his full weight pressing down on her, stopping her from making the slightest movement at all.

Helpless, wild-eyed, alarmed and disturbed, Elena looked up at him, and opened her mouth to scream—and he silenced her in the only way that, at that moment, he could. He silenced her with his own mouth, warm, hard, demanding, like the rest of him.

She stirred helplessly beneath him, suddenly aware that this, now, was the most potentially explosive situation ever. On a bed, alone in his house, with no one to hear, no one at all, and she in the flimsiest of garments, and he on top of her, aroused, angry—all-powerful. All man. His arms were on her arms, his hands locked with hers. And the treacherous, dangerous warmth surged up inside her, and now she knew it was too late to ask for mercy—even had she wanted to, which she didn't. The sun shone in through the window, cutting a path across the floor and bed, and she murmured softly, helplessly, lost in the wonder of the sensation of his exploring lips, waiting for the inevitable, wanting him now more than she ever had before. He ran his hands up her arms to her shoulders, raised himself slightly, gazed down at her with eyes darker than she had ever seen them before, the pupils dilated with passion, his whole face shadowed with his desire for her, then with a groan he slid his arms round her body and kissed her again.

She slid her hands up his strong warm back, feeling the muscles, taut and powerful, moved one leg to ease his weight, and said huskily:

'You're heavy, Gregor.'

He moved, shifted slightly, to one side, and stroked her body with a featherweight touch, her breasts, her waist, her arms, her shoulders.

'You are most beautiful,' he whispered huskily. 'You are——'

'Please—be gentle with me,' she murmured. 'This is——'

He moved slightly, eyes narrowing. 'What?' he seemed almost dazed.

She smiled softly, knowing, waiting. 'This is the first time——'

'*Chort!*' He rolled off the bed, icy sober, and yanked her to her feet. He was violently, suddenly angry. Elena stared at him dazed.

'You are a virgin?'

She was almost crying. What was it? What had she said? 'Yes,' she whispered.

'My God!' He stumbled away from her, over to the window. She ran after him, touched him, and he rounded on her, and she took a step back, bewildered, feeling that he might strike her.

'Gregor, what is it—— 'she was crying now, sobbing, afraid.

He turned and walked out, slamming the door violently after him. She was alone. She looked at the closed door, her whole body in torment, and heard no sound. Then she put her hand to her mouth to stifle the growing sobs of anguish. Turning, dazed, she stumbled to the bed and sat down, huddled in a little ball of misery, rocking herself back and forth, until the tears subsided.

CHAPTER EIGHT

She should have learned by now. Twice Gregor had rejected her. Twice he had hurt her. The first time she had vowed it wouldn't happen again; but it had.

Elena sat at her dressing table later that morning trying to repair the ravages of an hour's tears. She had bathed her face, showered, applied a cold damp flannel to her eyes and lain down for half an hour on returning home, and she felt a little better. The events in Gregor's house were a merciful blur, and that was how she intended them to stay. There must be something wrong with me, she thought. It must be me. It was a frightening thought.

She had no desire to write. She couldn't, that was all there was to it. She picked up a bath towel, a book, and her suntan lotion, and carried them out into the garden. She found a spot that was partially shaded, and lay down to read. Señora Bonita brought her out a cool drink of fresh orange juice and announced that she was going, and did Miss Kingdon require anything from the town? Elena thanked her and said no, arranged to pay her wages the following morning, and settled down again to read.

She had heard Gregor's car leaving when she was still in his house, and left herself immediately afterwards. It was peaceful now in the garden, and she sipped her drink, and allowed herself to relax, allowed the shock to fade away gradually. Señora Bonita had been full of curiosity about her forgotten key, but Elena had managed to explain very casually what had happened, then went on to describe the party, and gone up to repair the ravages of her stay at Gregor's.

Jerry would arrive at ten. She no longer cared if he was angry; she could cope. After what Gregor had done to her she could cope with anything. She hoped he might be sufficiently annoyed to punch the big Russian in the jaw, even considered the idea wistfully. He needed a good hiding. The only trouble was that Jerry, tough though he was, would hardly be a match for a man who looked as if he could fell an ox with one hand tied behind his back. Still, she could dream....

The telephone shrilled and she ran in to answer it. It was the American woman who had been at the Ellersons' party, Ellen Freeman, asking her to a party the following week. Elena thanked her, said she would be delighted, and noted it down on the pad by the phone. Then she dialled the Ellersons' number to thank her for the party. That task done, she went outside again and lay down. She must try and write later. She mustn't let him affect her life like this.

She fell asleep, shaded now, and was woken by

Negra bounding over to lick her face.

'Ouch!' She sat up and pushed him away. 'Oh, you silly dog!' He looked as though he had been swimming, and had left damp paw marks all over her towel and sundress. She laughed, exasperated. 'Now look at me!' Then she heard Gregor's voice calling the dog, and froze. 'Go on,' she whispered, and pushed him. '*Go!*'

In answer he barked delightedly as if it was a new game, and the next moment Gregor appeared through the trees. Elena turned, bent, picked up her book and walked into the house, closing the french window firmly after her. She stood inside and watched Gregor call the dog again, glance briefly towards the window, hesitate as if unsure whether to come and speak—and she willed him to go away. She didn't want to speak to him. He turned and went, followed by Negra. She gave him a couple of minutes and went out again. But her peaceful mood was shattered. She could no longer relax, in case he reappeared. It was nearly four o'clock. She went in, made herself a drink and some salad, and went upstairs to write.

Now the book flowed as never before. She amazed even herself. She had a meaty scene involving the villainous Count and a lady of the court —and the words sped along, almost of their own volition, across the page, filling it. She was tired, and her hand ached when it grew dark. But she had finished the first chapter, practically a record for speed with her. The chapter closed with the Count

getting a sound thrashing from an irate husband.
It was most satisfying. Almost as satisfying as the
real thing. . . .

She prepared a salad and chicken for Jerry and
went to wait for him in the lounge, curled up with
a book. He would be here soon. The window was
open, letting in a cooling breeze, very welcome after
the heat of the day. The room was comfortable, the
furniture old but good, and Elena had a glass of
wine at her side, and more waiting for Jerry in
refrigerator. She heard his taxi coming up the
drive, and ran to open the front door. Only it wasn't
a taxi. It was Gregor's Rolls, and both he and Jerry
were getting out, laughing like old friends. Jerry
turned, saw her, and waved. 'Hi, honey. Long time
no see.' He went up the steps and kissed her
warmly. 'Can Gregor come in? He's something to
ask you.'

'No,' she muttered, but Jerry was walking with
her, arm round her waist, into the hall, and Gregor
was following, and short of ordering him out, what
could she do?

They went into the kitchen, and Gregor said:
'Elena, I have a problem.' Oh, I know you have,
she thought, haven't we all?

'Really. What?' Her voice didn't drip icicles, not
quite, but near enough, and Jerry looked vaguely
startled.

'I am having urgent repairs done to the water
system at my house—may I sleep here for a couple
of nights?'

She gaped at him, genuinely lost for words, and Jerry added helpfully: 'He was telling me all about it when he met me. I said I knew it would be all right. Funny how everyone arrives at once.'

Very funny, she thought. Very, very funny—and fishy.

'There seemed nothing wrong this morning,' she said.

'No.' Gregor looked gravely at her. 'But when I came home after lunch the kitchen was flooded. I thought at first you might have left a tap on, but it was not that—some pipes have gone in the main water system. It also affects the air cooling system.' He shrugged. 'I hate to impose on you, of course, but in return I will supply all meals for us all this weekend. It is the least I can do.'

Jerry was looking at her, pleased, clearly unaware of the deep thread of force stretching between them, anxious only for everything to be nice and easy.

'Very well,' said Elena, because it was all she actually could say, short of screaming at him to get out. 'I'll go and see to a bed. What about Negra?'

'Could he come too?'

'Of course.' She didn't add, I'd rather have *him* than *you*, because she didn't need to.

'I'll go and fetch my clothes.' He turned and went out.

'Eat your salad, Jerry,' said Elena.

'What's wrong?'

She widened her eyes. 'Wrong? Good heavens, *nothing*. Why?'

'Oh, I thought you might think I'd be annoyed about you spending the night with him——'

'At his house,' she corrected smartly.

He grinned. 'Sorry. But then he explained,' he shrugged. 'He's a fine guy. I knew you'd not mind him staying. And I'll be a chaperon, won't I?'

'Indeed you will.' As will Gregor for you, she thought. And I wouldn't put it past him to have wrecked his own damn pipes—though why he should care whether I sleep with you or not, I can't imagine. 'Coffee, Jerry?'

'Fine, thanks. Hey, that's nice, isn't it? All our food supplied. No slaving over a hot stove for you for the next couple of days.'

'Lovely.' She heard Negra bounding in, and into the kitchen, clearly pleased, and Gregor followed with a weekend case. 'I'll take you up,' she said. 'This way.'

She went into the bedroom in between Jerry's and hers, and pointed to a chair. 'I'll get the bedding later.' She turned and went out, and Gregor caught her arm at the door.

'Wait, please,' he said.

She looked coldly at his hand. 'For what?' she looked up at him then, clear and icy.

'I have to speak to you.'

'No, you don't. You've said it all. Let me pass, please.'

'I must explain——'

'No,' she said gently, and took his hand away from her arm. Teeth marks showed clearly above his wrist. 'Did I do those? I'm so glad. There's really no need for you to explain anything to me, ever again.' She looked at him, and her eyes were very bright. 'Really, I'd rather you didn't. I've had enough humiliation for one day——' her mouth trembled, but she held her chin proudly high. 'Why don't you go down now and use your charm on Jerry, and as far as I'm concerned, we'll be just good neighbours. No scenes, I promise you——' and she walked quickly out before he could read what was in her eyes. She heard his indrawn breath, like a silent cry of pain, but she ran quickly down the stairs.

She made the effort, she really did. Her words, said to him, had done her good, cleared the air. She was the perfect hostess, and when Jerry had eaten they all went into the lounge, with Negra, and sat and talked. Gregor and Jerry went over to his house to bring back drinks and cigars, and while they were gone, Elena washed the dishes and rinsed out three glasses and found an ashtray.

They came back carrying not only the drinks, but a record and cassette player, and a stack of records and tapes. Gregor indicated them. 'Please, choose what you would like to play,' he said. 'That is, if you'd like music?'

'Of course.' She sat on the floor and sorted through, found a favourite Neil Diamond long-player, and put it on. The music filled the room,

Gregor poured the drinks, Jerry fetched ice, and the two men talked while Elena listened to the music. At eleven Gregor said: 'Are either of you hungry?'

Elena said: 'No,' but Jerry looked up hopefully.

'Well——' he drawled, then looked at Elena, who shrugged.

'I thought, if you were, I would phone the hotel and ask them to send some in.'

'Great!'

'Elena, are you sure?'

'If you're eating, I'll enjoy something,' she answered.

'Fine. May I use your telephone?'

'Of course.'

He went out, and they heard him dialling. 'Did the manuscript arrive before you left?' Elena asked Jerry.

'Yep. I only had time to skim through it before letting Gerrard have it. Did you type it for him?'

'Yes. Could you tell?'

'I could. Very professional. Elena.'

'It should be,' she smiled wryly. 'I'm a writer, remember?'

When Gregor returned she went up to make up the bed for him, and as she went down the car with the food was arriving. As before, it was packed in a box, with plates and cutlery, and a bottle of wine. Perhaps, she thought, he often does this. Gregor insisted that he would set everything out, Elena was to do nothing, and she didn't demur. It was different in that instead of chicken there was a large ham, but there was smoked salmon, stuffed avocado, and a strawberry cheesecake to finish off with.

She ate little, but enough, and said: 'I'm going to bed now. Stay up as late as you like, both of you. Goodnight.' She left them sitting at the table, patted a hopeful Negra, sitting by his master's side, and went upstairs.

She could hear their voices as she washed, but she couldn't distinguish the words. She wondered if they were talking about her, and if so, what they were saying. She lay for a while listening to the music drifting faintly up, heard the dog bark once, then fell asleep.

She had closed her door, and when she awoke in the middle of the night to go to the bathroom she nearly fell over Negra, who was sleeping just outside it. He looked up apologetically and moved aside. When Elena came back he was curled up on her bedside rug fast asleep. She looked at him. I wonder whose idea that was, she thought. The guardian at the door. She climbed over him, pulled the sheet up, and fell asleep.

When she awoke the dog had gone, and the hot sun streamed in through the undrawn curtains. She listened for a minute, but heard no sounds, went to the window, and saw Gregor's car had gone. Putting on her wrap and slippers, she went downstairs. There was a note on the kitchen table in Jerry's writing.

'Gone to San Cristobál with G,' she read. 'Back soon, love, J.' Brief enough. He didn't say why they'd gone. She didn't know how soon was soon, so she sat down after making toast and coffee, and had her breakfast. Then she went upstairs to get dressed and to write. Let them entertain themselves, she thought. It gives me more time for work. But she found herself listening, all the same, for the sound of his car, and it was a distraction she could have done without.

In the end she gave up trying and went down to hear them just arriving. They were loaded up with cartons, and both were laughing. She opened the door for them. They were like a couple of schoolboys let out of school, she thought, not grown men. Gregor had a deep laugh, infectious to hear, so she closed her ears to it and went into the lounge.

Jerry came in first. 'We've got the weekend's food,' he said. 'All packed away ready.'

'We're going to a party at the Rossis' tomorrow night,' she told him. 'I hope you can manage it. When do you go back?'

'Aw hell, midnight tomorrow.' He turned round as Gregor, who had come in while they were talking, said:

'No problem. I will run you from the party and go back for Elena.'

She might have known he would be going. 'Great. Fantastic,' said Jerry. 'What time's it start?'

'Nine.'

'That gives me a couple of hours. Okay, what are

we doing today?' And they both looked at her.

'Don't look at me,' she said sweetly. 'I've handed the weekend over to Gregor to organise,' and she smiled at him.

'You will leave it to me?' He inclined his head. 'Then may I suggest a few hours at the country club, returning for our evening meal?'

'Why not?' The country club had been there ten years ago, but Elena had never been. It was very exclusive.

'Take swimsuits. Jerry, may I loan you a pair of trunks?'

'Sure. That sounds fine by me.'

Half an hour later they were off, accompanied by Negra.

It really was, she had to admit, a superb place to spend a day. There were indoor squash and badminton courts, a large swimming pool, golf course and turkish baths. They spent the rest of the morning sunbathing and swimming, Elena played badminton with Jerry, and sat watching him and Gregor play squash. The club was moderately full, Gregor knew everyone—of course—and she recognised several couples from the party, and after lunch they sat sipping Bacardi and Coke on a secluded shaded terrace and watched the swimmers. Negra sprawled out under a shady palm and dozed the afternoon away, and Elena realised, much to her surprise, she was enjoying herself thoroughly. In part it was due to Gregor, who was charming, courteous and considerate to them both.

Elena lay back in her striped lounger and dozed, listening to the hum of voices in the background, the splashes and cries from the pool, and the distant drone of a plane. She was getting nicely tanned, and her brief black swimsuit showed her figure to perfection.

She heard them only vaguely say they were going for a swim, and did she mind, and waved them away. It was too much effort to move. She thought one of them had returned when a weight came down on the middle of the lounging chair and a hand touched her leg. She opened her eyes, ready to blast Gregor—if it was him—but it was a perfect stranger.

'Well, hello,' he said. 'You *are* real after all. I thought I was having a rather lovely dream.' He wasn't drunk, but he had certainly been drinking. Elena drew her legs away from him and smiled coolly.

'No, you're not dreaming,' she said. 'Excuse me, but I was sunbathing. Would you mind moving off my chair?'

'Would you mind moving off my chair?' he mimicked, and smiled. He was perhaps forty, tall, handsome in a rather flashy manner, dressed only in shorts, and she definitely didn't like him. 'Are you English? It's a quaint accent.' But he didn't move.

'If you're not moving, I will,' she said, and smiling sweetly started to get up. He pushed her gently down.

'Don't be so snooty,' he chided. 'I want to buy you a drink.'

'I've had one. Buzz off.' She turned her head. 'Negra!' this sharply. The dog opened his eyes, looked, and ambled over. He sat beside her and looked at the intruder with faint interest. Elena sighed. Clearly he thought this man was a friend, for he was sitting on the same chair. He wagged his tail.

'This your dog?'

'No. He belongs to a friend who happens to be swimming at the moment.'

'And he's left you alone? Shame. What'll you have? Gin—vodka—Bacardi?'

'Nothing, thank you. And take your hand off my *knee!*' she pushed his hand sharply away and Negra growled, no longer sure about the man, who stood up rather quickly and said:

'Prickly little thing, ain't ya?'

'I don't like pests. You're one. Leave me alone!'

'Sure, I'll leave you alone.' His face was flushed and he stood there, glaring at her, hands on hips. 'I was just trying to be friendly—you English are all the same, snooty pieces——'

'I don't like strangers putting their hands on my knees——'

Her antennae had let her down this time. Gregor's voice came, soft and deadly, from behind the man: 'Has he been annoying you?' and the man turned viciously, saw Gregor and took a step back, nearly tripping over Negra, whose fur rose on his spine.

'I merely asked her if she wanted a friendly drink,' he began, blustering, rather paler now.

'Well, she doesn't. And if you don't want a punch on the nose, I suggest you go and offer your drinks elsewhere.' Gregor didn't look angry, but he didn't look too pleased either. Elena watched the scene with interest. She held Negra's collar, more as a precaution than anything else. Let Gregor cope alone.

'Tough guy, aren't you? I mean, with the dog and all.'

'Yes. And I don't need the dog to help me. And if you don't move now, I'll get you banned from this club for life.'

The man's underlip went out. 'Oh *yeah*! You and who else?'

'Just me. I'm Gregor Vlados, and I'm one of the directors. Any more clever questions?'

'Aw hell, you don't——' the man moved suddenly, swung out at Gregor's jaw, and was sent sprawling by one of Gregor's giant fists. He hauled him up by his shoulders and held him firmly.

'You want another go?' he asked, deadly quietly, 'or are you leaving now?'

All the bluster had gone. The man, with a venomous look at Elena, walked off, holding his jaw.

Gregor looked down at her. 'I'm sorry that should have happened,' he said. 'Why didn't you shout for me?'

'Because I didn't know if you'd hear, and anyway——' she shrugged, 'I had Negra to guard me.'

He looked down at the dog and grinned. 'He didn't seem to be doing much when I arrived.'

'I didn't know the right words. The idiot dog thought he was a friend.' Suddenly she saw the funny side of it, and began to laugh. Jerry came up, dripping wet, said:

'Can anyone join in the fun?' So Elena told him, and he started laughing too. Gregor went off to get more drinks for them and Elena thought over what had happened, and remembered Gregor's face when he had knocked the man down. He had looked as though he were swatting a troublesome fly, no more. Almost casual. That was the power of the man. A quality of ruthlessness, necessary in business, but in private life? She bent her head and stroked the dog.

The heat shimmered off the white buildings, quivering the air, and the light was pure white and dazzling. Elena looked up to see Gregor returning, carrying a tray of glasses. She studied him, the athletic powerful build of him, the sheer perfection of masculine body, muscular, superbly fit, and her heart ached. She had to keep reminding herself that this was the man who had ruined her father, but that was getting more difficult to think about with each day that passed.

He crouched down beside them, passed Elena her long frosted glass.

'Thank you,' she said. He looked at her, briefly,

his strong face expressionless, eyes slightly narrowed in the dazzling light, and she wanted to touch him; she ached to touch him, to hold him. She looked away, out over the pool.

Dear God, she thought, I think I'm beginning to love him. With no rhyme or reason. Against every measure I use for judging character, against all I've ever known. She felt almost lightheaded with the sudden knowledge. It was essential to behave normally.

Jerry, dear Jerry, broke the taut thread that stretched between them. 'Hey, done any more writing, you two?'

'I've done a chapter,' volunteered Elena. 'You can have a look when we get back if you like. Let me know if I'm on form.'

'A chapter?' he gave a low whistle. 'The air must suit you. Keep it up. And you, Gregor?'

'I have had no time, but next week perhaps, I will. I would like to finish the book soon.'

'So would I—like you to, I mean.' Jerry grinned at Elena. 'Keep him at it, honey.'

'I'll try,' she smiled. She included Gregor in the smile, then lay back in her chair. 'Just now I don't want to think about work. I want to get a lovely tan.'

She closed her eyes and drifted, listening idly to them talking, discussing hotel work, and Jerry's business as a publisher, and she thought about everything—and most of all she thought about Gregor. Then she dozed.

Gregor woke her, and they were alone. 'Jerry has gone to have a turkish bath,' he said, 'and then we are leaving.'

'Don't you want one?'

'We are not leaving you alone again.'

She laughed. 'He won't come back.'

'No, but there might be others. Who knows? Do you want to go and change?'

'Mmm, in a minute. It's lovely here.'

'You can return any time you want.'

'I'm not a member.'

'As my guest. I will get a temporary membership card for you while you are on the island.' It seemed there was an unspoken question hovering in the air.

She said quickly: 'That's very kind of you. I might take you up on it.' Did he want to know when she would leave? I might never leave, she thought. I would not be alive away from you— and yet I cannot live near you, and see you with other women. You have altered my life, and you will never know it.

'Did you enjoy your lunch with Chuck yesterday?' she asked.

'Yes. It was a working lunch. He has a good administrative brain. I could use him in the hotel.'

'But does he need to work? His parents are wealthy, aren't they?'

'Yes. But they want him in the family business, and he's not interested.'

'Oh, what's that?'

'Oil.'

'What else?' she laughed. 'I'll bet they're from Texas.'

'Right.'

There was silence, and she wanted very much for Jerry to return. How simple it would be if I fell for Chuck, she thought. Then I could stay....

'I didn't know you were going to the Rossis' party tomorrow,' she said.

'You didn't ask me.'

'Isn't it rather odd you should go to two parties in one week, when you don't particularly like them?'

'No. Why?'

'Because Lois Ellerson seemed surprised you'd said you'd go—and she *seemed* to think it was thanks to me,' she said, and waited.

'Lois is a bird-brained woman. I am not responsible for her ideas,' he answered calmly.

'But——' began Elena, and stopped.

'But what?'

'Oh, nothing. You have an answer for everything, don't you?'

'Not always,' he answered quietly, and she felt herself go unaccountably warm. She looked at him, meeting his eyes, seeing into the dark depths of them, reaching into his very soul, aching——

She had to look away then, and he touched her arm, a feather-soft gentle touch. 'Look at me,' he said.

She turned slowly, her eyes dark blue, shadowed,

and looked at him. Then he smiled, softly.

'Why?' she said, simply.

'Because I wanted to see something, and now I have.'

'What did you want to see?' she felt breathless.

Gregor stood up. 'You. The real you.' He turned away. 'Here's Jerry.'

No, wait, tell me what you mean, she wanted to cry, but it was too late. Jerry flopped down, and the moment was lost for ever.

CHAPTER NINE

ELENA's refrigerator was crammed to capacity with food, and late that evening they played three-handed whist, then had a late supper of exotic sea-foods and salad and fruit. All were tired after the day at the country club, and when Gregor had taken Negra out for a walk they all went to bed. This time, because of the heat, Elena left her door open, and Negra came in as of right, curled up on the rug, and went to sleep. So did she, almost immediately afterwards.

She awoke very early, wide awake and refreshed after a sound sleep, and went downstairs very quietly, followed by the faithful Negra. 'Do you want to go out for a walk?' she asked, and was nearly bowled over by his enthusiastic, not to say ecstatic response. 'Come on, then.'

It was cool and still, with the remnants of dew fast disappearing from the grass. On impulse Elena took off her sandals and walked barefoot in the garden, tasting the cool air, breathing it in, relishing the quiet and stillness of the pre-dawn time. Both the men, her guests, would be fast asleep. She wondered what Gregor was dreaming about. Money? Women? Not her, that was for sure.

She put on her sandals and ran down the drive,

laughing at the odd sight she would present to a passer by at that hour, dressed only in nightie, negligee and sandals. Fortunately there were no passers-by. A crazy mood took her, she reached the gate and on impulse turned into Gregor's drive and ran up that. Negra ran beside her, tongue hanging out, keeping pace with her by merely loping.

Gregor had had the pool built since he moved in. Elena wandered round, curious to see it, looking at the closed, lifeless windows of the house she had once lived in—been happy in. She paused. Had she ever been happy there? Really happy? It was a disquieting question.

The pool was large, the water blue and still. Negra paused and sat down, waiting to see what she would do next.

'I'm going for a swim,' she told him. 'Okay?' he wagged his tail. Anything she did was presumably fine by him. She was totally alone, it was not yet seven, and nobody, anywhere, was awake. Elena, laughing at the mad impulse which had caught her, kicked off her sandals, took off her wrap and laid it over the wooden bench by the pool, stripped off her nightie, and dived in.

It was wonderful. After the first skin-tingling shock of immersion she revelled in the cool velvety water on her skin. She swam, floated, dived to the bottom and surfaced gasping, then she crawled two lengths with quiet dedication, timing herself. She'd never beat the world record, but then she wasn't trying to. It was glorious. In a minute she would come out, go home and dry herself, but just now she was alone in the world, and everything was far away, slightly blurred because she hadn't her contact lenses in, and it was more fun that way. She dived, surfaced, swam towards Negra—and saw the man watching her.

For a moment she couldn't see who it was, and sank down so that just her head showed, then her eyes focussed, and it was Gregor.

'What the hell are you doing?' he demanded.

'I'm swimming. Go away, I've no clothes on.'

'I can see that,' he retorted. 'You're mad!'

'I know—I don't care. Go away!'

He laughed. 'And if I don't?'

'Well, I can't stay here all day.'

'I can see you well enough now.'

'Oh.' She looked down at herself, and wondered if she'd gone pink all over. She swam to the edge where he waited, and stood beneath the shelving round the edges and looked up at him. 'Will you pass me my nightie, please?'

'No. Come and get it yourself.'

'Thanks! Negra, fetch!' She pointed to the bench, and the dog whined and cocked his ears, clearly trying to understand. She was getting cold, not moving. 'Look—*please* go away, then I'll come out. *Please!*' Her teeth started to chatter.

Gregor said: 'Wait a moment,' and went into the changing cabin. He came out with a large brown towel. 'You can have this.' He reached down and held out his hand to her.

'Close your eyes,' she begged.

'All right.'

'Promise?'

There was a silence. *'Promise?'* she repeated.

'No. I'm coming in for a swim.' He wore only his trousers.

'But you can't——'

'I can.' He began to unbuckle his belt, and in sudden panic Elena dived away from the edge. She remembered what had happened the first time they been swimming....

As soon as he dived in, she'd get out. She edged nearer the steps, casually, nervous, excited—and heard a splash. Instantly she swam towards the steps—and he reached them first. She didn't want to look, but it appeared that he might have nothing on....

'Jerry will be awake,' she said faintly, half turned away from him. 'Look, if he comes out now——'.

'Yes. He can join us, can't he?'

She struck away from him, swimming fast, but there weren't many places to go, and he caught her up and slid his arms round her. He was dark and unshaven, and she was frightened, and fell back from him, pleading now, 'Let me go,' but he answered:

'It's my pool. I do what I want in my pool,' and she wasn't sure if he was teasing and she didn't want to find out. Then he kissed her....

He kissed her, and it began again, only this time she wasn't going to give him the chance to turn away from her, to reject her. This time she was going to accept it as all part of the fun, on a light level—difficult but——

'Mmm, lovely.' She laughed, and kissed him back, then caught his head and ducked him hard so that he went right under, gasping and spluttering, and she heard her own laughter—then he grabbed her leg, from underneath, and pulled her down, down, and, underwater, he caressed her, and she was all his for a brief moment, then she was free, kicking away from him, splashing him, still laughing and breathless, and she reached the steps and clambered out and ran for the towel, reached it, and put it round her. Now she was safe. She stood well away from the pool and taunted him:

'Let's see you get out now!'

He did. Elena averted her eyes, scrabbled for her nightie and pulled it over her wet head, dropped the towel, wrapped her negligee round her and closed her eyes and held out the towel. She stood there primly, eyes tight shut, and said: 'Here.'

The tingle in her neck and head told her where he was, then she felt his warm, wet hands go round her, round her body, and she stiffened and tried to escape. His wet body was against her. She could feel the damp seeping through the flimsy material and she whispered:

'Go away!'

'When you have kissed me again.' His voice was muffled, in her ear, his hands were very much in control of her.

'No!'

'Then you stay like this.'

'And if I kiss you?'

'I will let you go.'

'Promise?'

'I promise.'

She turned, slowly, luxuriating in his touch, but with sufficient of her mind in control. She had learned that much since yesterday. She slid her arms round his damp neck, touched the wet hair, stroked it, and pulling him to her, kissed him. His face, his lips, were damp.

'Mmm, now I can go?'

'If you want to.'

She picked up the towel which had fallen at her feet, and wrapped it round him. Then she opened her eyes. 'Fasten it,' she said, and tucked it in. Then she tapped his cheek. 'Don't be late for breakfast. I'll let Negra come back with you.' She was laughing as she walked away to the trees.

She dressed herself, and she felt marvellous. Gregor hadn't returned, and she didn't care. She took a cup of coffee to Jerry, who was surfacing reluctantly from a heavy sleep, then went down to search the refrigerator. She was spoiled for choice, eventually decided on a fresh pineapple, to be followed by ham and eggs. She was grilling the ham when Gregor walked in.

'It won't be long,' she said. 'Did you enjoy your swim?'

'Yes. Did you?'

'It wasn't bad. You have a nice pool.' She looked at him. 'Why don't you go and shave before breakfast? You look a mess.'

He rubbed his stubbly cheeks and jaw. 'It can wait.'

'As you wish.' She turned away. 'I took Jerry up a coffee.'

'Did you? How fascinating.'

She raised her eyebrows. 'Oh *dear*, you're not very sunny this morning. Did you get up too early?'

She hummed a little tune as she turned the slices of ham under the grill, and broke eggs into the pan, then sliced the pineapple. Gregor quietly smouldered. She knew he was, and she didn't know if she was the cause, but she didn't really care. Once, for just once, she had, somehow, got the better of him, and she felt very good.

Jerry staggered down, yawning, and slumped down at the table.

'Breakfast won't be a minute,' Elena trilled, and he groaned.

'You should have gone for a swim,' she said. 'I did, and it was lovely.' She looked at Gregor, who said nothing. She made the coffee, gave them their breakfast, and sat down for her own. 'I'll let you two wash up,' she said, 'seeing that I wasn't really supposed to be doing any work this weekend. I'm going up to write.'

Gregor made the effort. She could see that it was an effort. 'If Jerry doesn't mind, I will do some work on my book too.'

'Great!' Jerry came to life. 'It's my bread and butter you're talking about, remember. I shall sunbathe in the garden.'

'Then that's lovely.' Elena beamed at them both. 'I'd appreciate a coffee round, say, eleven. Okay?' She took her plates to the sink, and went out.

For the rest of the morning, Elena wrote. A peaceful silence had descended upon the house. She didn't know where Gregor was doing his writing, and she didn't really care. When, at about eleven, a swimming trunk-clad Jerry came up with a cup of coffee, she told him:

'It's going well. Close the door after you.'

'I can take a hint.' He grinned, kissed her, and went out again, whistling. That's funny, she thought. He hasn't proposed once this weekend— and he doesn't seem the slightest trace jealous of Gregor. She stared into space, pondering that. In fact they get on more like a chummy pair of brothers —and *I'm* the odd one out. The one they put up with. It wasn't strictly true, but she enjoyed her short burst of martyrdom, shrugged, and got back to work.

The next time she was disturbed it was past three o'clock, and Jerry came up to tell her that he, and he alone, had prepared lunch, and she was to go down *now*, regardless of what she was doing, and she hadn't forgotten they were going to a party that evening, had she?

She hadn't. She went, she ate, she returned to

her work, and so the day passed.

Just after nine, they set out for the Rossis', leaving a sad-faced Negra behind to guard the house.

It was a rather boring party, and the excuse of having to see Jerry off on a plane gave them all a reason to leave at half past eleven. Uttering profuse thanks to their host and hostess, they made a grand exit, and escaped in the Rolls, to drive to the airport.

'I'll phone,' Jerry told Elena. 'I'll have to see when I can get down again—it'll be as soon as possible, but I've a lot on this week.'

'Of course, love.' She kissed him warmly. 'Just give me a couple of hours' notice.'

'And I'll phone you too, when I hear from Gerrard,' Jerry told Gregor. They stood in the departure lounge waiting for him to be called. The airport was a vastly different place at night, spectacular, floodlit, with the dark star-studded sky seen from the long window, remote and mysterious.

Jerry's flight was announced; he hugged Elena, shook Gregor's hand, and left them. They watched him enter the plane, saw it take off, then Gregor said: 'Let's go.'

'I don't want to appear rude,' said Elena, as they walked to where he had parked the car, 'but how long are you staying at my house?'

'Ah, yes.' He regarded her gravely. 'I was going to say—they will be commencing work in the morning.' He opened her door, helped her in, and slammed it shut. She watched him walk round. He hadn't answered her question.

'Yes, but how long will it take?' she persisted.

He shrugged. 'I do not know. I can, of course, go and stay in town at my hotel—is that what you wish?'

She knew suddenly that it wasn't what she wished. 'But,' he continued, 'knowing Spanish workmen I have to be on the spot to supervise—and I do not like the idea of you being all alone in such a remote spot.'

He had a point. 'I could get the Bonitas to live in,' she began, and he laughed.

'They have three of their sons still living at home. How could they?'

'Oh. I didn't know.' He was driving away from the airport now. 'But—well, what will people think?'

'They will not know, will they?'

'But——' she paused.

'I know what you are thinking. I will be a guest in your house. I would not abuse your hospitality,' he said gravely, and she was silent. I wouldn't like to bet on that, she thought. It seemed so logical and sensible. Everything he said seemed logical and sensible—and at least she had made herself clear. Or had she? Elena felt confused. But she knew one thing: she knew she loved him. His nearness hurt. His absence would hurt more.

'Very well,' she said. 'Stay until the work is done. I shall be busy writing most days, of course.'

'It shall be only for a few days, I will see to that. And I shall provide all the food.'

'Thank you.'

He drove swiftly home, and she thought, I shall be alone with him in my house. She was dicing with danger, but she had lived with safety for long enough. She smiled to herself in the darkness. Gregor had said no one would know, but Señora Bonita would. Perhaps she would give her a few days off. It would be easier for her own peace of mind. Then there would be no talk. Not that I care, Elena thought. Let people think what they like.

She sighed, and closed her eyes. Clever man, to have got his mistresses tidily out of the way for a while. She smiled to herself. She wondered what they were like. They would be beautiful; perhaps he collected beautiful women. She wondered if he had spoken about them to Jerry—if perhaps that was the reason Jerry didn't appear jealous. She must ask him some time. There would certainly be no point in asking Gregor. He was like a clam on certain subjects. As he said, no one will know. But he was wrong there. Someone did know—and Elena was to find out in the most unexpected and shocking way.

Gregor had gone when she woke next morning. He had left her a note on the kitchen table to say he would telephone her during the day, or call in. And did she mind him leaving Negra there? Of course she didn't. She enjoyed the dog's company. She took him to her room to write with her, found it was far too hot, and went down again to sit by the open windows of the lounge. From here she could hear the telephone more easily, as well. . . .

She placed a small table by the window, books on the floor, and began to write. Negra, after a small ramble round the garden, came to sleep at her feet. There were no sounds of activity next door, but then it was only ten o'clock. Perhaps they didn't start work until later. Perhaps they weren't going to start work at all; Gregor had seemed so casual about everything.

She soon got into the mood of the book. Count Igor really was coming along very nicely. The only trouble was, he was threatening to take the book over. He was not intended to be the major character, but was assuming the proportions of one. She wrote steadily on, sometimes so quickly that she knew she would have to re-read what she had done the following day before she began again simply in order to know what had happened. Such was the quality of the book. It had taken on a life of its own, the characters living, breathing people. Elena was like an observer, taking it all down, writing only what she saw. It was something new for her, and the feeling was in her bones, and it refused to go away, that this would be the best thing she had ever written. . . .

The telephone shrilled, and her heart leapt. Gregor—it must be him. She had never spoken to him on the phone before. 'Hello,' she said.

'It is me, Gregor. Do you know if the men have arrived next door yet?'

'I've not heard anything, Gregor. Do you want me to look?'

'No, do not trouble. I will call and see what is delaying them. Elena, I may be in very late tonight. I am sorry if it inconveniences you, but some urgent business has come up, and I have to attend to it. I do not like you to be alone, or I would stay at the hotel. Could you leave a key for me somewhere?'

'I could—but I'll wait up. The book's going so well I may write all evening, it's cooler then. Now I know, I'll have a rest this afternoon. It's really too hot. Er—as you're going to be late, I'll feed Negra, shall I?'

'Please. His food is in the back of the refrigerator in a large foil container. About half that with the meal biscuits.'

'Fine. Goodbye.'

'Goodbye.' She hung up and went back to writing with a lighter heart. It was a sense of anticipation. Silly, she didn't know why, but it was there. It was the thought that Gregor would be arriving later. Like a husband, coming home....

She laughed at herself for the foolish fancy, and Negra joined in by whining and wagging his tail. Elena hugged him. 'You're a lovely boy,' she said. 'Like your master!'

She rested after lunch, after paying Señora Bonita her wages for two weeks, and telling her that for the next few days she would be concentrating on writing, and would the Señora like a few days off? The Señora would, and seemed delighted, assuring Elena of her immediate return when needed.

Then after tea, and a leisurely stroll with Negra in the hilly, richly grassy woodland at the end of the gardens she returned and started to write. She put on a tape first of Gregor's, of Russian music, Borodin's *Prince Igor*, one of her favourites, and most definitely mood music for what she was writing. The hours passed swiftly, darkness fell, and she sat by the open window, perfectly content and safe with Negra to guard her, and let the words flow from her pen.

She heard no car; she was too engrossed. It wasn't until Negra ran out barking that she felt a faint twinge of alarm, which changed to relief when she saw Gregor loom up out of the darkness with the dog leaping round him.

'Oh! You gave me a fright——' then she saw his face. 'My God, what happened?' Three long bloodred scratches ran down his left cheek. He touched them.

'Those? A cat scratched me.' He laughed. 'I didn't realise they showed.'

'Have you put something on? You should.' He shook his head. 'I'll go and get you something.' Elena turned, ignored his comment that it wasn't important, and went into the kitchen for her personal first aid kit, which contained TCP ointment. There was no suspicion in her mind—not yet. That came as she smoothed on the yellow ointment. They didn't look like cat scratches. She went cold inside. It was nearly midnight. What was the business that had detained him—a woman? A woman—and an argument. She closed her eyes, feeling sick inside, and turned away. 'That's done. Do you want anything to eat?'

'No, I've eaten out. I need a drink, though.' She watched him pour himself a large vodka and drink it neat, and she swallowed. He rarely drank. Perhaps, after what had happened, he needed one.

Dear God, I don't want to know. *I don't want to know*, she thought fiercely, and found that she had clenched her hand so tightly that the nailmarks showed on her palms.

'I'll have a small one,' she said, and poured it. 'Then I'm going to bed.'

'Do you mind if I stay up a while? I would like to do some writing myself, and I am too wide awake to sleep.'

'Feel free. Use my table.' She cleared her papers away and put them in the bureau drawer. 'I've fed Negra, but he's not had a walk for several hours.'

'Thank you.'

'Goodnight.' She didn't look at him as she said it. She couldn't, she didn't want to see the scratches. She ran upstairs, and when she reached the top she put her hand to her mouth and choked back a sob. Her imagination was providing all too vivid pictures of how Gregor had spent his evening. But with whom? The fiery Mexican beauty, or the

American girl? Either might have returned. Or someone else? The third woman at his house?

I've picked a fine one to fall for, she thought, as she prepared for bed. A Casanova of the old school. Trust me! It was hot, but she locked her door. At least she would be sure of undisturbed rest that way.

When she awoke in the morning—much surprised that she had in fact slept—it was to hear the shower running. She turned over, prepared to wait until Gregor had gone down. The minutes drifted past and she planned her day. Writing, writing, and more writing. Perhaps out in the garden for part of the day. She needed a few items from the shops, but decided to ask Gregor to fetch them. It would save her going.

She heard the bathroom door open, and his footsteps on the stairs, waited a second, and got out of bed. As she locked the bathroom door she heard the telephone ring, and paused, waiting for him to shout for her. But he didn't. He spoke briefly. She couldn't distinguish the words, because he spoke very quietly, low-voiced. Then the phone tinged as it was put down. Elena pulled a face and started running the shower. He would tell her who it was.

But he didn't. When she went down he had prepared breakfast and was eating his own, fresh mangoes with cold cooked ham, an unlikely combination, but a surprisingly delicious one.

'What are you doing today?' she asked him, as she finished off with her traditional toast and marmalade. Gregor lowered his coffee cup.

'If it does not inconvenience you, I wish to write this afternoon. This morning I have to go out, but I'll be back for lunch. I shall bring that in. Will you leave it to me?'

'Of course. And you can write as long as you don't disturb me.'

He smiled faintly. 'I won't do that. How is your book coming?'

'Very nicely.' She hoped he wouldn't remember that she had told him she was going to use him. 'And quite fast. I'm happy about it—at the moment. But that's all I dare say. I might put a jinx on it if I talk too much.'

He laughed. 'Of course. I shall ask no more. May I bring you anything back from San Cristobál?'

'I want a few things. I'll make a list, okay?' Then she remembered something she—and apparently he —had completely forgotten. 'The dress!' He looked blankly at her. 'The dress I bought for the Ellersons' party. You were going to give me the bill.'

The scratches seemed very prominent, and Elena tried her best to avoid looking at them. 'I too forgot. It was not deliberate, I promise you. But please, reconsider now. I am using your house as my own. Will you not accept it as a gift for your hospitality?'

There was a moment's pause, a hesitation on Elena's part, and he added: 'It will make me feel less guilty.'

She couldn't imagine him feeling guilty about anything. 'Very well. Thank you very much.'

Gregor inclined his head. 'A pleasure.'

He went out shortly after and took her list, mainly personal items, soap and toilet water, talc and shampoo. It was quiet with him gone, and she wandered round tidying up, made her bed, peeped in his room to see it immaculate. He was a personally very neat man. There was a photograph of a woman on the dressing table, beside his razor and comb, and she picked it up. It was in a small silver frame. The woman was young and had a haunting beauty, and there was something vaguely familiar about the face. Elena frowned slightly. Another one? She replaced it carefully. Somehow, another one didn't make her any more jealous, She didn't understand why. Perhaps there was safety in numbers. She had to smile at that thought.

The telephone shrilled and she ran down to answer it. She had forgotten to ask Gregor who had rung before, and he had forgotten to tell her. She picked it up. 'Hello?'

'Miss Kingdon?' The accent was American. She immediately thought of someone she had met at the Ellersons' party. Another invitation coming up....

'Yes. Speaking.' She drew the pad towards her, and picked up the pencil.

'You don't kow me, but I know you. I know *all* about you.' She realised with a faint shock of horror that the woman at the other end of the line was shaking with anger.

'Who are you?' she said. 'Who is this?'

'Never mind. Just listen. Leave Gregor Vlados alone, keep out of his life—or I'll kill you, you two-faced, scheming bitch!'

CHAPTER TEN

SHE meant it too. Elena pulled up a chair to support her shaking legs, and said: 'You're either mad or sick. And if you don't tell me who you are I shall hang up and phone the police.'

'Like hell you will! I'll tell *you* something— you think you're clever, don't you? Boy, you think you've fooled him, but you haven't. He knows exactly who you are. Do you hear me? Exactly who you *really* are—Miss Elena *Shaw*.'

'My God!' Elena whispered. This was a nightmare. She was rewarded by a throaty laugh.

'That surprise you, honey? I thought it would. He's been stringing you along—you didn't guess, did you? He knows who you are, and he knows why you're here—he even made sure you would be. Why did you think your *uncle* left you that house? Not 'cos he loved you, that's for sure. 'Cos Gregor persuaded him to. Boy, have you been fooled! But the game's gone on long enough. It's past a joke. I want you to clear out of his life before I do it for you. I hope I make myself clear?'

Elena took a deep breath. Her hand was gripping the receiver so tightly it nearly broke.

'I know who *you* are,' she said, keeping her voice steady with the greatest effort of self control. 'You're

Loren Slinger.. I know all about you too.' The sharp indrawn breath told her she'd hit the target. 'You're pathetic! And as far as I'm concerned, you can go to *hell*!' and she slammed the telephone down.

But she barely made it to the bathroom before she was sick. She sat on her bed for a while to recover, while she thought about the implications of what the American woman had told her. It had the ring of truth simply because she couldn't possibly have made it up. That she had been talking to a dangerously jealous woman was also very obvious. So who do I ask for help, she thought, Gregor?

Gregor, who not only knew the truth about her, but had used his resources to get her here. For what purpose? There was only one—revenge. *He* wanted revenge on *her*. A continuance of the one on her father? Things were becoming clear to Elena now, little clues she had ignored, but now she could no longer. Uppermost was Gregor's autobiography, the first chapter of which she had not only read, but typed. The fact that he had lived in the South of France, near Cannes. That his father had had a restaurant. Elena's father and mother had also lived in the South of France, in Cannes. They had been in the restaurant business. And her father had known Gregor Vlados before living on Cristobál....

She put her hand to her burning forehead. And something else Gregor had said. She *must* remember. Something about his manuscript. 'One day, you will know why I have written it,' he said. That was it. It puzzled her at the time—and also frightened her, because of some deep significance in his words.

Then there was something else. Her brain was working remarkably clearly now. Odd how danger sharpened the wits. Before the Ellersons' party, when she had been protesting about him taking her, he had said something very strange, something she had neither understood nor wanted to understand. He had said: 'One day we will understand one another, and then you will know that you hated me without reason or sense.' He had walked out after he had said it, leaving her standing. And the time passed, and she could not ask him about it.

'Oh, my God,' she whispered. She had to see his manuscript again. It was important. She had to read it with new eyes—to see properly. He had more, as well. She must read it, because inside might be the secret she sought, the secret that would explain his own plotting to get *her* to the island. She stared wide-eyed at the window. He must not know, he must not guess.

She was in danger from Loren Slinger; she might be in more danger from him. She was cold, very cold, although the temperature was in the nineties. Where lay safety now? She was on her own, truly on her own. She had to think clearly. First, she had to read his manuscript. He would not be back until lunch. She had two hours....

She ran down and found the box where he kept his papers. With shaking hands she opened it, and everything fell out: the first chapter, and more, much more. Elena ran to the kitchen, made herself a cold drink, threw in several ice cubes, and ran back to the lounge. Negra sat by her side as she began to re-read the first pages, now searching for clues, not merely reading, and enjoying the force of the words, but seeking what lay in those lines that might. . . .

A shadow fell across the pages, and she looked up, screamed and fell back, scattering everything on the floor. Then she scrambled to her feet and backed to the door.

'What is it?' Gregor dropped the parcel he carried and strode towards her.

She found her voice. 'Keep away from me!'

'My God!' he looked at the scattered papers, then back to her. 'Elena? What has happened?'

She looked round for a weapon, but there was nothing. The scratches on his cheek were vivid, and she knew now who had done them. He had been with *her* last night. Loving, fighting—laughing about me? she thought.

She fought to keep calm. She was in no immediate danger. They had been alone often enough. His revenge was going to be more subtle than that. But what revenge—and how had he planned it?

'Please go—go now,' she whispered. *'Please!'*

'No. Not until you tell me——' he looked again from the papers on the floor to her. 'Something has happened, hasn't it? Something that made you want to read what I had written. Tell me.' When she didn't answer, he said it again. 'Tell me.'

'She phoned me,' she whispered. 'She told me——'

'Loren?'

'Yes.' She shrank back from him. 'She threatened to kill me——'

'She *what*?' he towered, icily angry. 'Elena——'

'And I w-wanted to read what you had written, to—to know why—why you——' a sob was wrenched from her, and she put her arms round her body as if to shelter herself from blows.

'Dear God!' Gregor had gone white. He looked as though he were in pain. 'Elena, you are in no danger from me. I swear it on my oath. Believe me. But you must tell me what she said.'

'You know—you must know what you told her——' She stopped, her knees trembling so much she thought she would fall. She stood against the door for support, and looked in agony at him. 'I was reading what you had done because I thought I might find out why. I didn't expect you back— not yet. You frightened me.'

'The last thing I want to do is frighten you. But I must know what she said. I must know what she plans—I did not know she saw so much——'

'She told me to keep away from you, that the joke had gone far enough. She knew my name. She said you persuaded my uncle to leave me this house so that I would come here——' Elena faltered as she saw his expression. 'She said she wanted me to clear out of your life before she did it for me. She said she would kill me if I didn't.'

He sat down slowly, and now, strangely enough, it was Elena who felt stronger. She walked towards him. 'I wasn't frightened of her. It was you I was frightened of.'

Gregor looked up slowly. 'The only danger you have ever been in from me was that I might make love to you,' he said very slowly. 'But that danger no longer exists.'

'Then why—why did you get me here? You did, didn't you? You didn't deny anything. '

'I know. I had my reasons.' He stood up. 'And one day I will tell you. Our immediate problem is Loren. She is a dangerous woman.'

'She doesn't frighten me.'

'She frightens me. Who do you think made these scratches?' He touched them. 'I met her last night to tell her it was all over between us.'

'Was it she who phoned this morning?'

'Yes. You heard? I didn't think you had heard.'

'Why—why does she frighten you?' She shivered. 'You're a man. You're not afraid of a woman——'

'Not for myself, but for you. You are alone here when I am not here—she knows you are here. Elena, I want you to move out of here today.'

'But where would I go?'

'To my hotel.'

'No, I'm not running anywhere. Why should I? I can keep the doors locked——'

'Please! '

'No.' She shook her head. 'All we have to do is tell the police——'

'She moved out of her flat this morning. I went round to check, after she had phoned, because she sounded very strange. She said she wanted to see me, but she wasn't there—I don't know where she is. She could be anywhere on the island. It is one reason why I came back early. Some instinct told me——' he paused.

'I can't run,' Elena insisted. 'We did enough of that when I was a child. But perhaps you know, don't you? Perhaps you know more than I?'

He answered very softly: 'Yes.'

'Then you must know that running away doesn't get you anywhere. And after I move to the Plaza, what then? Do I stay in, hiding myself, and never venture out except with an escort? Do I go to parties wondering if I'll get a knife in my back if I don't keep looking over my shoulder? And how do you think it would affect my writing? I like it here. I'm writing well. It's *right*, here. If I couldn't write, I might as well die. It's a part of me, don't you see, Gregor? And whatever the rights and wrongs of what you're going to tell me about my—my father—it doesn't make any difference to the main issue.' She lifted her chin defiantly. 'I'm not saying I'm not nervous, but I stopped running, years ago, when I grew up.'

Gregor was silent, then he spoke. 'Elena, you have spoken from the depths of your soul. You are brave, you have courage of the spirit, and that I accept. But forgive me if I do everything in my power to protect you, because I shall, and nothing on earth—nothing you could say or do, would stop me.'

'I didn't expect you to say anything else,' she said quietly. Tears glistened in her eyes, and he touched her gently on her chin, lifting her face up to him. His own eyes were dark and shadowed. A sense of rightness took her, and the stillness of the room was filled with a kind of glow that touched them both, linking them; then he bent and kissed her very gently.

'I salute you,' he said.

Soon everything else would be right as well, but that could wait. The immediate problem, Loren, seemed almost trivial to Elena.

'I'm hungry,' she said. 'I know it seems silly to be thinking about food at a time like this, but I am.'

'Good. You don't eat enough,' he said. 'Come, we will eat. Negra, stay and guard.'

They went out to the kitchen where Gregor told Elena to sit down while he prepared everything. She did so. She watched him deftly peel and dice mushrooms and tomatoes and sauter them in the pan. He produced giant scampi and put them to warm while he watched the other pan. 'You like cooking, don't you?'

'Yes. I was brought up to the restaurant life. I make a very acceptable crêpe Suzette. You must let me show you some time. It is my speciality.'

'No Russian dishes?'

'Several. Ah, beetroot soup——' he frowned as

she pulled a face. 'Wait and see, and beef Stroganoff, and a sweet with strawberries and meringue that will melt your heart——' he paused. 'And you?'

'Oh yes, I'm not bad. I'll make you *my* speciality one night.'

'Ah. And what is that?'

'Toad in the hole.'

He began to laugh. 'You are joking with me!'

'No, I'm not! I shared a flat with a Yorkshire girl once, and she was always moaning that no one in London knew how to make it, so I showed her.'

'But what is it? You do not eat *real* toads, do you?'

Elena began to explain, laughing, and soon the lunch was ready, and they ate in a companionable atmosphere unlike any she had known before with him. He was different. Once again she was seeing yet another facet of his personality. He had the constant ability to surprise.

But after lunch, when he had gone into the garden to write and she sat by the window, she watched him. He had gone to see Loren the previous night to tell her it was all over between them. Why? And how many did that leave? Somehow, at that moment, it seemed more important to have the answers to those questions than to the other, unspoken ones that still remained between them. Questions about herself, and her family—and about his reasons for getting her there on the island.

While Elena prepared their evening meal, Gregor asked her if he could use the telephone. She heard him faintly through the closed door. He was on the phone for quite a time, and she guessed that his calls had to do with Loren. When the food was ready, and on the table, she went to tell him. He was speaking quietly. '——I see. Thank you. Yes, I'll be in.' He put the telephone down.

'The food's ready,' she said, and he turned towards her.

'She hasn't left the island,' he said, walking towards her. 'I checked with the airport. I've also phoned others. If anyone sees her, anywhere, they will tell me.'

'Then where could she be? Surely she's over-dramatising the situation? I mean—good heavens, she must have known she was one of many——' She faltered slightly at the expression on his face, but she had had enough of evasion. 'I've heard enough about you and your women to know that.'

'Have you?' His mouth quirked slightly. 'I wonder what you have heard?'

'Does it matter? It's true, isn't it? I'm not stupid. You're a man who—who needs women——' She turned and walked to the kitchen and he followed.

'Please continue.'

'We'd better eat first.' She sat down. It was easier, sitting down. She didn't have to worry so much about her legs shaking. His face was grave. Not angry—not yet. She had seen his anger, and it frightened her. She didn't want him to be angry, because she had had quite enough for one day. She picked up her fork. 'I've seen you with them, remember? Everywhere you go—*she* must be used

o that, so why is she so jealous of me when I'm
not even——' She bit her lip, and Gregor said,
before she could continue:

'Because she knows that for the last two years I
have followed your every move, have known all
about you, and your travels, and your books—
everything. *That* is why.'

CHAPTER ELEVEN

His words weren't making sense; they just didn't make any sense at all. How could he have followed her every move when he didn't know her? She was white, and almost dizzy. 'I don't understand,' she whispered.

'You will. You remember going to New York when your first book came out?'

'Yes.'

'I was there. I had known you were going to be there—your uncle Jim had told me. I lied to you, Elena, about him. I knew him well.'

'You've lied about a lot of things,' she said bitterly.

'No. A few—necessary—he was a sick man. He was a recluse, but not to me. He was a very bitter, unhappy man, and he told me everything about his life, and that of your family, over these past ten years, when I got to know him. I was sorry for him at first, it was more pity than anything, I admit, and while you think I am a hard, ruthless man, I have a heart. We talked, we got to know one another, and I began to feel affection for him, because I realised why he was like he was. What I am going to say now may hurt you— he had had to mortgage this house to pay your father's gambling debts——'

Elena rose from the table, pushing her chair back. 'No—stop!'

'You must listen if you are to understand.' His voice was harsh. 'I helped him. I gave him money. This house was mine—it was I who arranged for you to have it. Did you never wonder why it was not left to your brother, or to you both jointly? Because it was you I wanted here. *You.*'

'But why? Why me?' she cried.

'Because of that evening I saw you in New York, on television, being interviewed over your book, and I knew there was something I had to do. I was waiting outside your hotel the next day—part of a crowd. I made sure you didn't see me. I didn't know if you would recognise me again. You had changed, physically, but I hadn't. You were now a beautiful woman, no longer the little schoolgirl who had hated me, whose hate had shown in her eyes so that I could never forget it as long as lived. I knew I didn't deserve that hate, because you didn't know the truth, and I did. So I vowed there and then that one day, I would make you see.'

The food on the table grew cold, untouched, forgotten. Elena sat down again, and pushed the plate away from her. 'Your book,' she whispered. 'Is that——'

'That is a part of it, yes. It is for you. It is written entirely for you. Do you think I care if it ever gets published? There is only one person I have written it for, and thanks to Jerry, it was certain you would read it. It was to tell *you* the truth. You, and no one else. That was my plan, to get you here, to make you see, so that you would know that your hatred was falsely based. I have thought of little else over these past two years—no, ten.'

The words fell into the silent air, and Elena, hearing them as though from far away, looked at him blindly, scarcely seeing him, her whole body trembling, her mind dizzy with a sharp awareness of what he was saying. Ten years: the length of time she had loathed him. And now he was trying to tell her something so deep, so profound, that she had scarcely the understanding to grasp it. She put her hands on the table to steady herself.

Her voice came out in a faint whisper. 'The book—it tells the truth, doesn't it?'

'Yes.'

'And—is it about—my father?'

'Yes.'

'Dear God! The connection—in the South of France, before we came here—it is about that?'

'Yes.' Gregor stroked his jaw. She saw that he was white, and his hand trembled. The tension that filled the room was awesome and terrifying, yet there was no going back. Nothing could be unsaid. He rose to his feet, came over to her, and touched her shoulders. 'Come into the lounge. We can't talk here.' Weakly she allowed him to lead her out from the kitchen, his hands supporting her —or she might have fallen.

She sat on the settee, and he sat beside her, leaning towards her.

'Your father ruined my father. I came here seeking vengeance—I came here with the express purpose of ruining him in return, and I succeeded.'

'No——' she shook her head from side to side, moaning softly. 'No!'

'Yes, that was my code. He took my father's life—when he ruined him, my father killed himself.' His voice was dark and bitter. 'I swore on his deathbed that I would see justice done. I promised my mother. It took me seven long years of working all hours of day and night I could to save the money—I nearly killed myself in the process, but the one burning ambition conquered all else. Then, with my savings hidden in my one small case with all my possessions, I worked my way across on a freight ship, and arrived in Cristobál.' He paused. 'I already knew about your father's insatiable lust for gambling. He was already heavily in debt when I arrived. If you like, he helped me to accomplish my purpose. I rented a small shop and I worked night and day, single-handed, to alter and rebuild it. Then, with a staff of one, I opened my restaurant. I was gifted—I knew that. I had been taught by the best chef in the world—my father. That was his one legacy to me. The restaurant I opened was three doors away from your father's. I took most of his customers away from him within a month. Within three I had the tourists and locals queueing up outside. I had extended the premises by then, and I had taken three of his best staff. I was on my way up, and he was on the way out. But I had done nothing underhand—I had not used your father's methods.'

Elena put her hands over her ears. 'No—I can't hear any more——'

'You must.' Gregor took her hands and pulled them away. 'You must hear the rest, then you will know.'

She gazed at him, anguished, the pain showing in her eyes. 'It's my father you're talking about. My *father!*'

'He was a cruel, ruthless man——' She jerked herself away from him and stood up, trembling.

'No!' as he stood, 'don't come any nearer!'

'He paid people to cause scenes in my father's restaurant. He *paid* men to say they had found cockroaches in the——'

'No!' she screamed. 'How can you say——'

'I followed one out one night—after the damage was done, after several couples had walked out vowing they'd tell everyone—I followed him, to where he lived, waited for him, and made him tell me. I beat him up, I nearly killed him, so help me —but I found out the truth. Only it was too late then. The damage was done. All the little things that had mounted up——'

'My father couldn't have done that!'

'He *did*. He was up to his eyes in debt. You didn't know that, did you? He gambled all your mother's money away—he nearly killed her——'

'*You* did. She was dying when we left here——'

'Of a broken heart. Jim told me——'

'I won't listen,' she sobbed. 'You're hurting me!'

'It hurt me when my father killed himself—it hurt my mother—it broke her heart. She died months later——'

'Oh, God!' The cry was wrenched from her, and Elena sank down to the floor. Gregor pulled her to her feet and held her to him. Her whole body trembled. Helplessly she clung to him, unable, now, to move away. 'It's true, isn't it?'

'Yes, every word. On my life. But you—you were an innocent child, and that I could not bear. I would have given anything not to see the hatred in your eyes. And I knew then that I owed you something.' He drew himself slightly away so that she could see his face. 'I owed you the truth.'

He was supporting her, holding her, and she didn't want to move away. On a long, shuddering sob, she said: 'Hearing the truth, at last, I—knew —I think I knew, all along, that something was terribly wrong with our life. Nobody ever told me anything, and I was frightened and unhappy. In a way—over these past ten years—I've been trying to forget that part of it, because it was too much to bear——'

'Your brother knew,' he said softly. 'He left home, didn't he?'

'Yes.'

'And your uncle. He knew, and he was saddened. He knew everything, but he still tried to help your father. That is why I helped him. He was a sick man, all alone. He had been loyal—and had had his reward. I am deeply sorry, Elena, that I had to tell you like this—I would have preferred that you found out gradually, but Loren's behaviour changed all that.'

'Was she—your mistress?'

'For a time, yes. But it was all over months ago. Before——' he stopped. 'She came back at the week-end, unexpectedly, because someone had sent her a cutting of your arrival. There were no strings on either side. She knew that when I first knew her, knew too that the relationship was purely physical. I saw her last night. We had always agreed that we led our own lives—I knew she had other men, but I was not jealous. I never have been, of anybody.' His eyes were dark and grave upon her. 'Until recently.'

'And Juanita? Another?'

Gregor smiled. 'You have been doing your home-work, haven't you? No, she wasn't, never has been my mistress. But I enjoyed her company, and I bought her gifts—she was happy with the arrange-ment, so was I.'

'And—the other night—the woman in your house?'

'Ah, her! Yes,' he smiled slightly. 'I will intro-duce you to her. She is seventy—and deaf.' Which probably explained why she hadn't answered Elena. But it didn't tell her *who* she was. 'She used to be my housekeeper, then retired about a year ago. She went to live in a small apartment in my hotel, and had left a trunk of clothes at my house—I took her there to collect them that evening, because she was going to live with her married granddaughter in Mexico. That is all.'

'And the photo on your dressing table?' Elena whispered tremulously.

'My mother, when she was your age.' That then was the likeness which had puzzled Elena. She didn't know why she was asking, except that it took her mind from other, far more disturbing things.

'Let me sit down,' she said.

'Of course.' He knelt before her. 'Forgive me,' he said quietly.

She reached out to touch his head. 'I know that you spoke the truth—in everything. There is nothing to forgive, is there? I've hated you for ten years, but I don't any more. I don't think I hated you from—from the moment I saw you in the Plaza, the day I arrived.'

He took the hand that she had resting on his head and kissed the palm gently. 'Do you know why I saw Loren last night?' he whispered.

'You told me——'

'Not why. I didn't tell you why.' He looked up at her, and it was all in his eyes. 'It is because there is no longer any room in my life for another woman. I once told you that I had never met any woman with whom I would want to spend my life. That was true—then. It is no longer true.' He groaned, and laid her hand along his cheek, holding it there. 'I think I have loved you for two years, Elena. Say that you do not hate me.'

'I don't hate you,' she whispered. 'I should have —I thought I should have, but I don't. I love you.'

He pulled her to her feet, and kissed her. It was a long, slow, tender kiss, tremulous, aware. Then he looked at her, his eyes dark. 'You are my life now,' he whispered huskily. 'You are the breath in my body, my heartbeat, my love. I shall never let you go. I will never be away from you, not for the merest second, for you are me, and I am you——'

'I don't want ever to be apart from you,' she answered. 'How can I? You are a part of me now, and always will be. If you leave me, I would die, it's as simple as that.' She reached up to touch his beloved face, and the power of their love filled the room—then Loren walked in through the open french windows, and stood there.

They turned, and looked as they heard the cry of pain that was wrenched from her, but Elena was not afraid. She never had been, but now, in the circle of Gregor's arms, she was safer than she had ever been before in her life. She looked across at the blonde beautiful woman, and felt only pity.

Gregor spoke: 'There is nothing here for you, Loren,' he said. 'You must go away.' They were united, and it was like a potent force stretching round them, reaching across the room to touch the watching woman, whose face was contorted with hatred. And she knew. She knew, and she seemed to shrink away, to become smaller, even as they watched. She put her hand to her mouth.

'You cannot hurt Elena, or me.' Gregor walked away from Elena, and towards the woman. 'It was all over between us a long time ago. You know it— you've known it for a while—why don't you accept it?'

'Because it wouldn't have been if she hadn't come,' she screamed. 'I could have made you love me——'

'Like you made Todd love you? Or Brent—or any of the others?'

Loren shrank back. 'Who—told you?'

'I made it my business to find out. Let's not kid ourselves. I was not the only man in your life—I haven't been, ever. Good friends made sure I knew all about you, presumably so that I wouldn't make a fool of myself over you, but I had no intention of doing so. Nor had you, over me. That was clearly understood all along. And now you'd better go. I don't like you threatening Elena. You may threaten me as much as you like, but I will have you run off the island, and I will make sure you never work as a beauty consultant here or anywhere in the States ever again—and believe me, I can do it—if you ever come within five miles of Elena again.'

He stopped in front of her. 'There is a plane ticket waiting for you at the airport, and there is a plane at midnight. You have four hours. I suggest you are on the plane. There is no work for you, and there is nowhere for you to stay, on Cristobál.' He stood before her, towering, powerful and relentless. 'And in return I will make sure your Kentucky

financier—Grant Tyler is his name, I believe—
doesn't find out about your little threats.'

Loren's face was ashen. She looked across at
Elena. 'You're welcome to him!' she spat. Then
she turned on her heel and walked out. Gregor
closed and fastened the window, then came back
to Elena.

'I'm sorry, my darling,' he said. 'I had to be hard
on her. We won't see her again.'

'I know.' She shivered. 'Please don't ever be angry
with me. I don't think I could bear it.'

'How could I be angry with myself? For that is
what it would be—I would only hurt myself.' He
put his arms round her. 'There is still one thing I
need to explain.'

'No,' she whispered, for she knew what it was.
'You don't need to——"

'I do,' he whispered fiercely. 'I must. You told me,
that morning—it was true, wasn't it? No man has
ever——'

'Yes, it was true.'

He gave a deep sigh. 'When we make love, for
the first time, it will be when we are married. Do
you understand what I am saying?'

'Yes,' a mere breath of sound.

He smiled faintly. 'It will be difficult to wait,
but you will see how strong I can be. When—how
soon—can we be married?'

'How soon can you get a licence?'

'Tomorrow?'

'Then tomorrow it will be. Gregor, is there really

anything wrong with the water pipes at your house?'

He began to laugh. 'Do you want the truth?'

'Of course.'

'No. I had to flood the kitchen myself in case you checked—and I let Negra paddle in it——' she began to laugh helplessly. 'I was not having Jerry staying here alone with you. Do you blame me?'

'Not now I don't. But you could go home tonight if you wanted,' she said demurely.

'Yes, but I'm not going to. I am staying here with you. I have already told you, you do not go out of my sight ever again—*ever*.'

'But——'

Gregor silenced her with his mouth. 'Not ever,' he said fiercely, when he had kissed her. 'I think I want to go for a swim.'

'Now? Before we eat?'

'Now.' He opened the lounge window and they went out, laughing, into the darkness, leaving a puzzled Negra guarding the house.

Elena's voice floated back from the garden, 'But we've forgotten our costumes——' and was cut off abruptly. Silence fell.

Negra, bored, lay down and rested his head in his paws. He hoped they wouldn't be long.

Harlequin Omnibus

The collected works of Harlequin's world-famous authors brought together in the 3-in-1 Omnibus.

3 Full-length romance novels in each entertainment-packed volume

Three great romances, COMPLETE and UNABRIDGED— by the same author— in one deluxe paperback volume . . . almost 600 pages of great reading.

A Great Idea! Harlequin Omnibus. We have chosen some of the works of Harlequin's world-famous authors and reprinted them in the 3-in-1 Omnibus. Almost 600 pages of pure entertainment. A truly "Jumbo" read.

Harlequin Omnibus

**The Harlequin editors have chosen this
superb selection of volumes from the works
of the Superstar authors of Romantic Fiction:**

Complete and mail this coupon today!

Harlequin Reader Service

In U.S.A.:
MPO Box 707,
Niagara Falls, N.Y.
14302

In Canada:
649 Ontario St.,
Stratford, Ontario.
N5A 6W2

Please send me the following Harlequin Omnibus volumes. I am enclosing my check or money order for $2.75 for each volume ordered, plus 49¢ to cover postage and handling.

☐ Catherine Airlie 2
☐ Nan Asquith 1
☐ Mary Burchell 4
☐ Mary Burchell 5
☐ Iris Danbury 2
☐ Iris Danbury 3
☐ Joyce Dingwell 4
☐ Joyce Dingwell 5
☐ Lucy Gillen 3
☐ Lucy Gillen 4
☐ Margery Hilton 2
☐ Pamela Kent 1

☐ Flora Kidd 2
☐ Roberta Leigh 1
☐ Roberta Leigh 2
☐ Rachel Lindsay 2
☐ Margaret Malcolm 3
☐ Margaret Malcolm 4
☐ Betty Neels 4
☐ Betty Neels 5
☐ Henrietta Reid 2
☐ Hilary Wilde 2
☐ Violet Winspear 4
☐ Violet Winspear 5

From time to time we find ourselves temporarily out of stock of certain titles. Rather than delay your order we have provided an alternate selection area on this order form. By indicating your alternate choices, we will still be able to provide you with the same-day service.

Alternate Selections _____

Number of volumes checked _____@ $2.75 each = $ _____

N.Y. and N.J. residents add appropriate sales tax $ _____

Postage and handling $ _____.49

                                    TOTAL $ _____

NAME _____

                        (Please Print)

ADDRESS _____

CITY _____

STATE/PROV _____   ZIP CODE/POSTAL CODE _____

Offer Expires June 30, 1979.   AB ROM 2267